Mrs. J. H. Riddell

Home, Sweet Home

A novel. Part 2

Mrs. J. H. Riddell

Home, Sweet Home
A novel. Part 2

ISBN/EAN: 9783337043704

Printed in Europe, USA, Canada, Australia, Japan

Cover: Foto ©Andreas Hilbeck / pixelio.de

More available books at **www.hansebooks.com**

HOME, SWEET HOME.

A Novel.

BY

MRS. RIDDELL,

AUTHOR OF
"GEORGE GEITH," "TOO MUCH ALONE," "THE EARL'S PROMISE,"
ETC.

IN THREE VOLUMES.

VOL. II.

LONDON:

TINSLEY BROTHERS, 8, CATHERINE STREET, STRAND.

1873.

LONDON :

SAVILL, EDWARDS AND CO., PRINTERS, CHANDOS STREET,
COVENT GARDEN.

CONTENTS

OF

THE SECOND VOLUME.

———

HOME, SWEET HOME.

CHAPTER I.

WE LEAVE LOVEDALE.

NO sentence passed all day between me and my grandmother concerning Miss Wifforde's visit. That lady and she had, so I afterwards ascertained, been closeted together for full half an hour before the former appeared at my bedside. I know now that in her magnanimous confession to me of wrong-doing, Miss Wifforde shot the last arrow her quiver held; but not even that arrow touched my grandmother's heart.

She was respectful. What Motfield had ever failed in due respect to a Wifforde?

She was sorry—the ties and associations of over sixty years cannot be severed without a pang—but when her visitor tried to reopen the question of education, so far as it concerned me, Mrs. Motfield stopped her.

"I have been thinking over what you said yesterday, ma'am," she began quietly; "and although I have never thought that in our station much book-learning was needed to fit a girl to be a good wife and mother, still no old-fashioned notions of mine shall stand between Annie and her education."

"I am very glad to hear you have arrived at that decision," answered Miss Wifforde. "Though, indeed, I expected nothing less from so sensible a woman as yourself."

"But," proceeded my grandmother, un-mollified by this compliment, "the more I think about your very kind offer, the less I think Annie ought to be allowed to accept it, even if she wished to accept it, which I am thankful to say she does not——"

"She did wish it up to a certain point,"

interrupted Miss Wifforde. "She left me full of pleasure and gratitude one hour, and returned the next, to say she could not leave you. Her whole proceeding was so strange and ridiculous, that I confess I lost my temper, and made some observations that I now exceedingly regret, ánd for which I beg to apologize."

"No need for that, ma'am," replied my grandmother; "only you must let me say —hoping no offence—that I think there is nothing strange or ridiculous in a girl wanting to stay with a person who has filled a mother's place to her. I am old and homely, I know, Miss Wifforde; but I believe if Annie were a young lady, and had thousands a year, she would love me all the same."

Here my grandmother broke down, a lump in her throat stopping farther utterance; and here came Miss Wifforde's opportunity. The likes and dislikes, the affections and hatreds of the " lower orders," were matters to which she had never paid the slightest attention ; in which, indeed, to put the fact plainly, she had very slight faith. And therefore, taking advantage of this momentary weakness, she harked back to her original position, and commenced once more a fluent recital of all the advantages—moral, physical, social, and educational—which must infallibly ensue from a few years' residence at Miss Brundall's select establishment for young ladies.

It was the same story which had once deceived my grandmother, repeated in a different form ; but this time it had no power to delude her understanding.

Well enough she comprehended it was from no love of me Miss Wifforde desired that advancement, social and moral, of which she had spoken. Although my tongue failed to reveal the mystery to her, she understood that " our ladies" wanted to be rid of a girl they considered dangerous.

Poor people are not always so incomprehensive as great folks think them.

They can be, if they choose, demonstrative to an extent, but they can also be obtuse to an equal degree.

No marvel that Miss Wifforde, who had been always accustomed to the cry and subservience of the poor who live by begging, did not in the smallest degree comprehend the proud humility, the haughty reticence of a nature that, having found itself once seduced by specious words, had with one effort torn itself free from the tempter for ever.

Very patiently she allowed Miss Wifforde to recite her parable, then she said—

"You are very kind, ma'am, and I thank you most sincerely; but if it would do Miss Cleeves harm to associate with my granddaughter, it would do harm to the other young ladies (like Miss Cleeves) at Miss Brundall's; and I do not want to hurt any one. I know, ma'am," she went on, "what

you would say—that Annie there would be
in a different position to what she is here ;
but I could not have my child looked upon
anywhere as a dependent without a dependent's wages."

"Your views have changed materially
since yesterday afternoon," remarked Miss
Wifforde.

"You did not give me time to think
yesterday," was the reply. "I did not
quite understand what it all meant, and I
was afraid of letting my selfishness spoil
Annie's future. When she came home last
night, with her face as white as death, and
her eyes swelled with crying, and told me
we should have to leave this place, I could
guess without another word from her
within a little of what had happened."

"But you could not seriously imagine
I meant what I said," exclaimed Miss
Wifforde.

There ensued an awkward pause. On the
one hand, my grandmother had still too

much respect for her visitor to retort that she believed Miss Wifforde had uttered every word of her threat in terrible earnest at the time it was spoken ; on the other, she was not a woman to tell a falsehood in the interests of politeness. Accordingly, she adopted a third course, and evading direct reply, said quietly—

" At any rate, ma'am, I intend to leave this place. When in your goodness you and your sister consented to let me end my days here, you could never have thought that what has come to pass was likely. I do not want to be a trouble to you, ma'am, or to let Annie be a trouble either, and so we will go. It may seem a little hard at first to make a new home at my time of life, still I am not afraid but that what is best for my grandchild I shall feel is best for me too."

Then at last Miss Wifforde was touched. She could not choose to be other than affected at the idea of an old woman, who had lived all her days in Lovedale, grown to its soil like a tree, whose memories were centred in the place, whose dead lay mouldering in its churchyard, going forth to a strange place among a strange people, for no cause or reason except that a little girl had come between the wind and her nobility.

Almost with tears she implored my grandmother to do nothing hastily. Without for a moment attempting to conceal that Miss Cleeves' partiality for me had caused serious annoyance to herself and her sister, still she declared they would rather the intimacy continued than that Mrs. Motfield should leave the neighbourhood.

" Nothing," she said emphatically, "could give me such pain as your going away." And I believe she only spoke the truth. She had a dread of the real cause of our departure becoming known. She feared the comments which might be made on the fact, that not all her authority had prevailed to keep Miss Cleeves from associating with the grandchild of old Farmer Motfield. She would have given, I doubt not, a thousand pounds cheerfully at that moment to have been rid of me ; but to be rid of me, with the chance of a social exposure of the whole of the circumstances supervening, was more than her equanimity could endure.

The longer she spoke, the more pressing she became. She said she would appeal to Miss Cleeves' good sense and good feeling. She promised to be a friend to me always. She declared she was really fond of me, and that my attachment to my grandmother had sensibly touched her. She offered that Miss Cleeves' masters should, at her own cost, attend at the cottage to give me lessons. She signified her desire to present me with a pianoforte. Never before had a Wifforde so pleaded to an inferior, but she might as well have held her peace.

My grandmother was obstinate, after the fashion of her age and class. After a struggle, in which she had uprooted all old associations, all cherished memories, her mind was made up as to the expediency of leaving Lovedale.

The happiness of her home was destroyed. Could she, at the bidding of this woman —Wifforde though she might be—tell Peace to dwell there ever again? Her feelings had been outraged, her pride insulted, her independence attacked. Could she forget these things, and, seated at her window, look up at the Great House calmly and admiringly as before?

No; as well might one who, in a fit of fury, had torn up the flowers in some fair garden, tell the owner to replant the withered roots, and make the desert blossom again as of yore.

She could not recall her threat; she could not unsay her words. In her passion she had come down from her pedestal, and in my grandmother's eyes she could never occupy it again.

In the watches of the night, the woman she had so bitterly grieved decided there was but one course for her to pursue ; and having decided, not all the Wiffordes who had dwelt at the Great House since time immemorial might have altered her determination.

As a last resource, Miss Wifforde bethought herself of making up friends with me ; and, confident in her own strength of will, my grandmother offered no objection to her desire.   She only said—

" I have not yet told Annie that I mean to leave Lovedale.   Please, ma'am, not to mention it."   And only too pleased at the tidings, Miss Wifforde promised discretion.

Perhaps I was more ill than she expected to find me.   Perhaps the interview just ended had really, as she said, touched her. No doubt she was very genuinely sorry for the threat she had used towards me ; at all events Miss Wifforde, so far as manner went, was tenderness itself.

" Poor little girl," she said, in answer to my sentence chronicled at the end of the last chapter, "have you been fretting yourself about my thoughtless and unkind speech ? Child, I would not drive a cat from its accustomed hearth; and do you think that, even were it in our power to be so cruel—which it is not, for Mrs. Motfield had our promise that she should live here always—my sister or I would break up the home of a person for whom we entertain so high an esteem as we do for your grandmother ? Keep yourself quiet, and when you are quite well again we will see whether we cannot manage to have you taught music at all events without leaving Lovedale." Then, and she smoothed the sheet over me and kissed my forehead and patted my shoulder, just as she might if I had been about five years of age, " Good-bye, my dear," she finished, " and get rid of your headache."

Then, as she passed out of the room, I heard her whisper to my grandmother, " You noticed what she said ?"

" Yes, ma'am," was the stiff reply ; " Annie is very fond of Lovedale."

That same evening, without my knowledge, a letter was despatched to Mr. Isaac Motfield, Parade, Fairport, which, after stating that it left the writer in good health—and trusting it would find himself and his wife and their children in the same—proceeded to set forth his mother's desire to have some talk with him on business. She did not, in so many words, request him to come unaccompanied by Mrs. Isaac ; but no one who read the epistle could have failed to see that he would be more welcome alone than otherwise.

For which reason, Mr. Isaac Motfield, to whom the postman handed this letter across the counter, never said a word about it to his wife, but took an opportunity of saying to her, that one of his customers, who was going to Uptons, a farm some six miles from Lovedale, had offered him a seat, and that as there was not much doing, he thought he would take the opportunity of running over to see his mother.

"I wish you could have taken Tommy," suggested Mrs. Isaac; "the poor child wants a change sadly; I cannot think what is the matter with him."

"He never could walk from Uptons to Lovedale," answered her husband.

"Well, you might tell grandmamma that he is very ailing, and perhaps she will ask him to spend a few days at the cottage," said Mrs. Isaac, who considered that life could hold no greater pleasure for any human being than the society of her progeny.

In justice to my uncle, I may here mention that the facts of Tommy's indisposition, and that his mother thought a change of air might prove beneficial, were duly mentioned, without, however, eliciting the desired invitation.

In truth, my grandmother's mind was at the moment occupied by much more important matters than Tommy's fit of indigestion. It was no small resolution she had taken ; it was no light work she was about to put in hand. Never shall I forget the astonishment depicted in my uncle's face when first she mentioned her intention of leaving Lovedale.

We were seated round the little tea-table, which was covered with many dainties in honour of our guest. We had so few visitors that we did not know how to make enough of one when we got him. It was a lovely evening, and the windows of the Great House seemed all ablaze in the light of the setting sun.

Not a sound broke the stillness. Not a cow was lowing or sheep bleating. The very pigeons were quiet. Not a creature was stirring on the road, and the general silence seemed to have communicated itself to us, for we drank our tea and ate our toast almost without exchanging a word, until my uncle said—

" Well, mother, and what is this weighty business concerning which you wish to talk to me ?   I suppose Nannie knows all about it, as she does about everything else ?" and he laughed as he laid his hand on my hair and stroked it kindly.

" Annie knows nothing about it yet," she answered ; " but there is no reason why she should not be told now.   I mean, Isaac, to leave Lovedale."

" Oh, no, grannie," I cried ; " no, no, no." Whilst my uncle, about to help himself to another portion of cold ham, dropped his carving knife and fork with a great clatter, and looked at his mother as though he really believed she had lost her senses.

" Yes, Annie ; yes, Isaac," she said, in answer to my remonstrance and his asto-

nishment. "Sit down, Annie, and do not
make yourself ill again." This to me
specially, for I had risen in my despair
and stood wringing my hands, and crying
out, "It is all my fault; it is all my
doing."

"You hear what your grandmother says,"
remarked my uncle. "Be a good girl, and
do as she bids you. Now, mother," he
added, "please go on. You took my breath
away for the moment, but I have got it
again. What is the English of what you
said just now?"

"The English is precisely what I said.
I mean to leave Lovedale."

"And how long have you come to that
determination?"

"Only the night before last; but I
wonder I never arrived at it before, seeing
it is the only thing to do."

"Why is it the only thing to do? and
why is it necessary to do anything?"

"Because Annie and I have agreed not

to part company ; and if she ever is to be educated in the way people seem to think she ought, it is high time we left Lovedale."

" So it has come to this at last," said my uncle, pushing his plate from him, and plunging his hands deep into his pockets, whilst I began to exclaim that I never wanted to learn anything more ; that I would rather be a dunce all my life than leave Lovedale.

Across this lamentation my uncle cut ruthlessly.

" Be quiet, Nannie," he said, more sharply than I ever remember hearing him speak to me before. " This is not a matter for you to decide. It is not a question of liking or disliking. It is what will be best. Mother," he went on, turning to her, with a jealous quiver in his voice, " how fond you are of this child, fonder than you ever were of one of us !"

" Don't say that, Isaac," she answered ;

"remember all I had in those times, while now——"

"You have but the one ewe lamb," he finished, "and I don't grudge the love you bear it."

"No, you need not," she replied; "for my age would have been very lonely without Annie. But finish your tea, my son," she went on. "And, Annie, when you have done yours, run away for half-an-hour. I want to have a quiet talk with your uncle."

"I cannot eat anything more, grannie, thank you," I answered; and after putting my chair back against the wall, as it was the rule to do in our methodical and unfashionable abode, I left the room.

Before I entered it again the business on which my grandmother had summoned her son to Lovedale was finally settled.

We were to leave the cottage; we were to go to that vague and far-away home where my father had died, and which had now been vacant for nearly twelve months.

My uncle was strongly of opinion that, considering the circumstances under which the Misses Wifforde had first offered his mother the free tenancy of our cottage for life, it would only be equitable for them to allow her to sub-let it, or give her such an amount annually, or in a lump sum, as might compensate her for its loss.

"Say what you will," he remarked in my hearing, "it is the people at the Great House who have brought this change about, and it is quite right they should pay for the indulgence of their whims, not as a matter of favour but of justice, and I shall see Miss Wifforde on the subject."

To this proposal my grandmother made no objection. Whatever her feelings may have been, she was not a woman to allow sentiment to elbow prudence out of any question she chanced to be considering.

For many years afterwards my own conviction was, that rather than have accepted a shilling from one of the Wiffordes, I would have cheerfully begged my bread.

Experience, however, modifies a vast number of convictions that young people are apt to think unchangeable, and I see no reason now to doubt the soundness of my uncle's judgment.

The Misses Wifforde, after vainly attempting to change the decision at which mother and son had arrived, frankly acknowledged the righteousness of my uncle's claim. They would have been more than just—generous—had he accepted their first offer; but he wanted and would take nothing beyond what he considered fair; and so it was ultimately settled that the cottage should be taken off our hands, that Mrs. Motfield should be paid twenty pounds a year for life, and that if she wished to dispose of her small farming-stock by private contract, they would take it off her hands at a valuation.

When all this was arranged, and my

uncle about to take his leave, Miss Laura Wifforde hinted a hope that the reasons which had no doubt largely influenced Mrs. Motfield's decision would be kept in the background.

"You may rely upon our discretion, madam," answered my uncle, who was quick enough of apprehension ; and then both of our ladies were graciously pleased to thank him very much, and they condescended to offer him a jewelled hand apiece, which he had no alternative but to take, looking, I doubt not, very much confused and ashamed the while ; and so he came away, and we were discreet to an extent.

Not from us did any one ever hear the true cause of that hurried removal ; not to the wife of his bosom did Isaac Motfield whisper the real truth ; but yet within a month from the time of our departure the whole countryside knew that Widow Motfield had left her cottage because the Misses Wifforde could not keep Miss Cleeves and

Annie Trenet—Farmer Motfield's grand-daughter—apart.

Miss Cleeves was not long in forming her conclusions when she came back 'to the Great House and found the humble nest it looked down on empty; neither was she reticent in expressing her opinions on the subject.

No entreaties or commands could tie her tongue; and I have since had reason to believe that the Misses Wifforde would not have objected to quadruple the modest annuity they paid my grandmother could they only have put things as they were before, and restored to their cottage its former tenant, who was to see Lovedale no more.

CHAPTER II.

MADAM MORRISON'S VERDICT.

T was all over. The old home was empty; we were trying to get accustomed to the new.

How other people may feel, I do not know; but to me nothing seems so difficult as to break the associations connected with, and to forget the memories that have gathered about, a place where one has lived for years.

On unwonted hearths the fires never seem to blaze the same welcome as of yore; in unaccustomed rooms the household gods look strange and unfamiliar. The attempt to make ourselves at home in a new house is like trying to gaze with favour on the face of one woman, while the heart is sick because of the love it still bears for another. So at all events we found the experiment; and though we tried to seem cheerful, I know the struggle was at first severe.

Cowslip's pasture in the trimly fenced paddock was richer than she had ever tasted at Lovedale, and yet the creature could not make herself content, but kept lowing at each corner of the field, as though a calf had been unjustly abducted from her; knee-deep in straw was our pony's stall, well-filled his rack and manger, nevertheless he persisted in whinnying for the well-remembered stable in which his youth was spent; mutely our dog, aged and almost blind, would lick our hands at intervals, as though in sympathizing recognition of a trouble and a change he was too old perfectly to understand; whilst Jill went about her work in depressed and solemn silence; and Jack whistled no more of those airs for the performance of which he had once been famous.

The only creature about the place, biped

or quadruped, who seemed perfectly happy, was our cat.

People talk about cats being attached to place; for my own part I do not think place is in the smallest degree material to them, if they can only lie roasting themselves in front of a good fire, if they have an abundant supply of milk, and ample opportunities for thieving. Our cat, at all events, accommodated herself to circumstances with a sweet serenity. When the sun was shining, she basked in his beams; when the wind blew chilly, she ensconced herself beside the best fire, wherever that fire happened to be. In the confusion of unpacking, numberless chances of annexing provisions occurred, and altogether my lady waxed fat, and went about in a rich sleek coat, whilst all the rest of us were trying to reconcile ourselves to the change as best we might.

But, of course, this state of mind could not last for ever; and accordingly, after a time, we ceased to think so much of the picturesque beauty of the Love, and addressed ourselves to consider the calm sweetness of the stream that strayed through the village where we had made our new home. In my heart I believe my grandmother really compassed more enjoyment of life in that village than she ever did in the dear cottage we had left, and to this hour it comforts me to think so.

At Little Alford she was somebody : at Lovedale she was at best Farmer Motfield's widow, an appenage of the Great House. At Little Alford she was in some sort a relative of the (reputedly) rich old lady who had lived, for forty years, or thereabouts, in the house, we took to, covered all over with ivy and roses and wisteria and magnolia

And it would be vain to deny that my grandmother liked and appreciated this consideration. Never in my memory had she exhibited herself in such spruce attire, in such snowy white caps and belongings, in such preternaturally black dresses.

She visited, and she received visitors ; she left more of the domestic management to Jill than I could have imagined consistent with her ideas of economy ; she still rose early, but not so early as formerly ; she still looked closely after household affairs, but they did not bound the whole of her horizon, as had been the case at Lovedale.

In her old age she took the recreation of which her younger and middle life had been so destitute. Is there no enjoyment, do you imagine, ye juveniles, for those whose cheeks are worn and furrowed ? On the contrary, with competent means and modest wishes, that, it seems to me, is the happiest life-period of all. It is babyhood without its helplessness ; youth without its restless aspirations. The ceaseless cares and the desperate struggles of an olden stage are past and forgotten, like the memory of a tempest on the sea. Over smooth waters the storm-tossed vessel glides peacefully into the last port she shall ever enter; and let the first part of the voyage have been what it liked, the latter is calm and pleasant.

It was so with my grandmother, at all events, God be thanked! There came a time when we could talk of Lovedale to each other without a break in our voices; there came a time when, other interests supervening, we rarely spoke of Lovedale at all.

At first I seldom went to sleep without being awakened by the dream-sound of plashing water and cawing rooks; but eventually even that link between me and my past broke altogether.

Yes; we were both very happy at Alford. By the time Cowslip had settled to her pasture, and our pony become reconciled to his stall, we were at home in our new abode. It was a larger house than that just left;

but our ideas had grown also. Even although it was all her own doing, had my grandmother lamented over Lovedale, after she had left the place, a shadow of sorrow must have rested upon me. As it is, I shall never think of those latter years save as years of pleasantness. I can never feel other than grateful for the sort of warning I received not to separate my lot from hers.

Apart we were in some things, apart far as the Poles; but then, which two amongst us, friends, are quite of one mind ? On this, however, we were agreed—we loved each other with a love deep, lasting, unselfish; and how much of my grandmother's new serenity was due to the pleasant society of Alford, and how much to the fact which was gradually dawning upon her understanding, that I should not eventually have to be a comparative pauper if I did not secure an eligible *parti*, I shall never comprehend thoroughly here. All I know is, she seemed a different woman.

After a time she not merely tolerated the sound of a secondhand piano, with which a judicious professor had furnished me, reserving to himself the usual commission, but actually grew to like its tones.

She never complained of the hours I devoted to practice, of the mode in which I pored over French verbs and essayed to make acquaintance with the sweet Italian tongue.

At Great Alford, two miles distant from our home, there was a school as famous in its way as that of the Misses Brundall, and thither three days a week, blow high, blow low, sunshine, rain, snow, or hail, I trudged regularly. Two miles—what was that to a girl of my habits? Two miles along lanes overarched by elm-trees; two miles between hedges laden with cob-nuts; two miles along white frosty roads; two miles with yellow primroses and budding thorn marking the way. Stories had I of my schoolfellows to bring back to our new

abode ; something always to report of what
I had seen on the road to and from Great
Alford.　It was altogether a new, but to us
a picturesque and pleasant life ; full, in a
small way, of people, and interest and incident.　The greatest trouble I knew was
that my voice grew suddenly weak, and I
was counselled not to attempt to sing much
at a time.

" Miss Trenet is growing fast, and she is
delicate," remarked the lady who taught
Do-Re-Mi to such pupils at Alford House as
paid extra for the attention ; " and in consequence her vocal organs are not strong."

Considering that I was extremely short
for my age, and that I scarcely knew the
meaning of ache or pain, Madam Morrison's
conclusions may safely have been declared
drawn from insufficient premises.

Indeed, she knew as little about physio-
logy as about music, which is saying a
great deal.

All this happened many, many months

after our removal to Alford. With that reticence which belongs, I think, to the possession of any gift, I was chary of saying I could sing.

Authors, as a rule, keep the secret of their first book as carefully as a girl does that of her first love—and in like manner it was a trial to me to speak of my gift at all.

The world has since acknowledged I had a gift; and therefore I may now speak of the matter with the same want of reticence as obtains in biographies; but I felt diffident and modest about the matter then, and had a reluctance to show my treasure.

For which reason many months elapsed after we left Lovedale before the question of my having or not having a voice was raised at Alford House. And the way in which it came to be raised at all was this: Uncle Isaac, in one of his pleasant letters, said—

"I am glad to hear Nannie gets on so

well in French, but you say nothing about her singing. How is this?"

How, indeed! I had been glad enough to put that matter on one side, whilst my grandmother certainly could have wished it forgotten for ever.

But she entertained a certain respect for her son's opinion, and remarked consequently—

"Annie, you had better speak to Madam Morrison." And I did.

I told the principal of Alford House, with many blushes, that if I had a talent for singing, my friends wished me to cultivate it, and she repeating this statement to Madam Morrison, I was invited to sing something for the lady.

Never worse in my life did I sing; I can state that fact positively; and it did not therefore in the least surprise me to hear Madam Morrison simper—

"A sweet voice, without much compass."
And then Mrs. Mitchell looked at me

blandly through her double eye-glasses—I always notice how fond respectable and dull-brained women are of mediocrity—whilst I, turning hot and cold, and red and white, in the same moment of time, and remembering how my song had once possessed power enough to compel the very linnets to stop and listen, was obliged to hold my peace, and look in silence at the light-haired idiotic woman, whose singing made me sick, and whose stupid incompetency I hated with an intensity worthy of a better cause.

I had been day pupil for a considerable time at Alford House when this little scene took place, and I had learned in the time to understand tolerably accurately the extent of Madam Morrison's musical knowledge, and the value of her critical opinion—still the faint praise with which she damned my vocal powers mortified me bitterly.

The praise of a wise man may fail to give pleasure, but the censure even of a fool

never fails to cause pain ; and as I walked
back to Little Alford I felt that this world
was not a nice place in which to live, and
that Mrs. Mitchell's select establishment
was an especially disagreeable corner of it.

All in vain I tried to console my self-
love, and flatter it back into confidence
again.

All in vain I recalled the bitter cold of
that immense room ; the out-of-tune con-
dition of the grand piano, on which Madam
persisted in playing an accompaniment, and
playing it all wrong ; my own excited and
nervous state of mind : my soul refused to
be comforted.

In fancy I heard again the weak, reedy
tones of my own voice; I had failed sig-
nally, and I could not help mourning bitterly, as I thought over my fiasco. It
seemed as terrible a matter to me as some
great loss does to a merchant, or a scathing
criticism to an author. I knew then, in my
heart of hearts, that I had been proud of

my voice—that I had been silently and secretly cherishing an idea of one day becoming a great singer. I understood suddenly precisely what I had long desired; and I comprehended at the same time why I never dared to give expression to that desire even to myself. I had wanted to use my own talent, although the force of surrounding circumstances kept it hitherto hidden away; and now, when there seemed a hope of my wish being gratified, I was told there was no talent to put out at usury.

Practically, that was the opinion Madam Morrison expressed; and though I did not believe in her judgment, still my faith in my own powers was so shaken, that I walked on humbled in spirit and sad at heart.

" Whither away, Miss Annie ?" said some one close behind me, when I had worked myself up into a very paroxysm of despair. " See what it is to be young; I am almost out of breath trying to overtake you;" and the doctor of Little Alford, one of the pleasantest and dearest of old bachelors, shook hands with me; and then, looking sharply into my face, said—

"Been in disgrace, eh?"

"No, sir," I answered.

"Then what is the matter? what have you been fretting about? If you spoil your eyes now, you will never be able to read without glasses when you come to be my age. That is right; I like to see you laugh. Now tell me what the trouble was."

I could not resist his kindly tones, his bright cheerful face, and told him my trouble, which seemed to become insignificantly small when laid out in words.

"Got no voice, Miss Annie, or next to none," he repeated, briskly; "that may be or may not be; at all events, we wont accept Madam's judgment as final. And so, you little puss, spite of your quiet demureness, you have been fancying you might some day become a second Catalini? Well, we have our dreams. When I was a young fellow studying medicine, I made up my mind I would be Court Physician, and the greatest man in my profession; and yet, you see, I am happy enough now, though only a country doctor, bound to listen patiently to the account of every old woman's ailments. But we wont despair of the voice, or of your being a great singer yet. By the way, how does it happen, if you are so given to carolling, that I have never heard you lift up your voice; no, not even in church?"

"I do not think my grandmother—that is—I mean, she may be afraid——"

"Afraid that the bird may not be content to stay all its life in a cage," he said, helping me out. "Well, there is something of wisdom in her notion. We will have a little more chat on this subject again. Meantime, don't spoil your eyes. Come over and see us, as often as the

French verbs and exercises leave sufficient leisure. My sister is always glad to have you. She says you are a good, quiet little girl; for my own part, after the revelation I have heard to-day, I am inclined to think you a small but very grievous hypocrite. Yes, you may laugh, but it is true. Good-bye, my embryo *prima donna*. I shall come to your benefit; remember that."

And he went on his way across the village green, whilst I turned into our home and told my grandmother what Madam Morrison had said.

"It is very odd," she remarked; but a sigh of relief escaped her even as she spoke. Almost unconsciously she had feared that, if I really possessed the gift of song, I might one day endeavour to turn it to account.

She would not have cared about my becoming a governess or a companion, or anything of that nature befitting my station and sex; but the very idea of my ever singing in public was a misery to her.

Of course, if I had no voice to speak about, that danger might be considered past. She would not mind my taking lessons, if it were impossible for me to make an improper use of the knowledge thus acquired. In her heart I believe she blessed Madam Morrison. She had never seen that lady, but as she was a teacher of singing, of course she must know whether or not I had any capabilities.

That was a happy evening for my grandmother, but she took care to conceal her exultation from me, as I took care to hide my disappointment from her.

With the first streak of daylight next morning I was out of bed. Before I fell asleep on the previous night, I had made up my mind as to what I should do; and accordingly before breakfast I walked a long way off, to a very solitary spot well known to me, where were no houses and no people.

There to myself, no one listening, I sung

my trial song; there, through the clear bright frosty air, I let my voice go free. I could still sing; I was satisfied. I did not care now for Madam Morrison, or Madam Anybodyelse; and I walked back to Little Alford as one might who treads enchanted ground.

CHAPTER III.

MY NEW FRIEND.

AN evening in the golden summer-tide; that is the time. A long low room with French windows opening into a large garden; that is the place. A lady, two gentlemen, and myself; these are the actors; and the question under consideration is an interesting one to me.

It may be summed up in the words Dr. Packman has just addressed to his visitor, of whom I shall have more to say presently.

"Well, Droigel, was I right or was I wrong? Has our small friend a voice? can she sing?"

Herr Droigel, a large man, with an immense acreage of fat cheek, on which not even a vestige of whisker could have been discovered, first looked at me with slow blue unwinking critical eyes, and then turned his gaze on Dr. Packman.

"Miss has a voice, and Miss can sing," he answered, in solemn tones that implied more than they actually said.

"Bravo!" cried the Doctor. "Did not I say so, Dorothy?" (This to his sister.) "Did not I say, that bitterly cold afternoon, when, as I told you, I overtook Miss Annie, who had been crying, I believed there was something in our little neighbour?"

"Yes, Decimus, you did," agreed Miss Packman, who, like her brother, was a charming member of society. I thought so then. I have seen nothing in society to make me change my opinion since.

Very calmly Herr Droigel waited till brother and sister had finished their little duet, when he resumed, as though his previous sentence had been left incomplete.

"But Miss will never make one grand success."

"And why not, pray?" inquired the Doctor.

"Why not! you ask, why not! and you a Doctor! Look—see—judge for yourself."

And he pointed an immense forefinger at my unfortunate person.

"Well," said Dr. Packman, "I look, I see, and I judge for myself. Why should she not be successful?"

"Stop, stop, my friend!" cried Herr Droigel. He pronounced stop "stope;" but as no form of spelling could ever indicate his accent, I prefer translating his speech into English. "You run on too fast; you are so full of—what you call it?—mercury. You pick me up half way. I did not say Miss would not be successful; on the contrary, I only told you she would not be one great success."

"Do you mean that she is not tall enough?" asked the Doctor, bewildered by distinctions that seemed to him to be without a difference. "She has plenty of time before her, and may develop for aught we can tell into a Siddons, as regards figure."

"Develop, pah!" repeated the German, with an expression of intense disgust. "You may grow high, so much" (indicating something seven feet or thereabouts), "and you may grow stout, so—like me" (spreading out his arms until a fearful physical diameter was suggested); "but can you alter this?" and he tapped his head, "or this?" and he laid his hand affectionately on his heart. "There is the artiste mind, there is the artiste body; mind or body, can you discover the artiste in this young lady with the divine voice?"

"Artiste fiddle-de-dee!" exclaimed the Doctor, contemptuously.

"I beg your pardon," said the other, pursuing his subject calmly, as though he were delivering a lecture; "it is not fiddle-de-dee; it is fact. Of some people in this world friends say they will plod along; they may earn, as your charming adage has it, ' salt to their bread,' but no butter—no, no, no, not one scrape of butter; and yet in a few years they have climbed the tree of fame ; they are able to shake down apples for the less fortunate to pick up. Of others, friends say, ' Oh, they will make one coup ; wherever they open the page, History will place her mark.' And what happens ? you ask. Ach, himmel !" with an ineffable shrug. " No coup comes, but a tumble, and History forgets to mark the page where their names are not recorded. Now, Doctor, attend ; now, Miss Annie, please to listen to an old man, an old man who has heard, oh, so many Miss Annies sing their little songs. If Miss Annie had the presence of a Cleopatra, if she had the genius of a Rachel, the grace and beauty of Grisi, the voice of an angel, she would never make one grand success. She will make, I trust, what is much better—herself a very happy woman. Some are born to be happy, and some to be great. For me, I think it is best for a woman to be happy, and not great. Oftentimes I say to my Gretchen, 'Mein Gott, how I thank Thee this child has no gift!' Sometimes I am forced to think Gretchen is less satisfied with the arrangements of Heaven than her father," he added reflectively, dropping his huge body into the furthermost recesses of an easy-chair.

"But, Herr Droigel," I said, speaking for the first time in my own interest, blushing scarlet as I did so, and feeling the hot blood tingling to my fingers' ends, "if I have a voice, and try to make the best of it, why should I not have a chance like others?"

"Because, my goot child, you are not like others; because you could never come to me and say, 'I have one father and one mother; I have sisters, I have brothers. I have said good-bye to them all; I mean to make one great success. When I have made it, I will remember father and mother, brothers and sisters ; but till then Art is my father and mother, my home, my sisters, my brothers.' Look, Doctor Packman," he added, rising suddenly and turning me towards the light ; " is that the brow of a woman who shall find her happiness before the scenes ? Should you wish those eyes ever from the footlights to scan the galleries ? Can you vision to your own imagining this child painted—powdered ? Pah ! Let us go into your churchyard and dig a pit, and bury her deep and safe, before such misery come to pass. And yet what a voice she has !—sing again once more."

There is a little Irish air, not so much known as it deserves, called, " Cushla ma chree."

In my very childish days I had heard it crooned by the wife of a man who came from the sister isle to seek work at the Great House.

She had a sickly infant, and in the noontide heat we let her sit under the shade of our elder-tree, and gave her food and drink ; and often afterwards, during that harvest time, she begged leave, in her soft sweet tongue, to rest awhile, praying a blessing on my grandmother for her goodness.

Thus it came to pass I learned to hum the air with which she hushed her baby. Subsequently I found in an old book words that some unknown poet had wedded to the music, and it was this song I essayed when the Professor bade me sing for him once more.

I was nervous no longer. I threw my soul into the melody. Like everything else I had ever learned from ear, I could sing it with all the tenderness and feeling I was at that time capable of expressing. As I went on, there mixed with the story of the love song a vision of Lovedale—of the old forsaken home—of the days that could never come back. For the moment

I was again looking on the familiar scenes
—the elder-tree cast a shadow over the
woman, her child, and myself—it was she
who was singing, not I—and then it ended,
and some one spoke.

"You shall be one ballad-singer," the
German said, rising and addressing me in
a frenzy of broken English. "I will take
you—I will teach you—I will perfect
that voice. You shall give yourself to
me. Yes, I, Droigel, will present you
to the world. You shall go with me to
London——"

"No, oh no!" I interrupted.

"And wherefore 'oh no? Am I a monster?
am I, as you say, hobegobelin? do you
think I want to make one meal of you,
Miss Annie? My dear, if you mean to
do good with yourself, you must do what
I tell you. It is one thing to sing pretty
and small and nice, to two, three people
in a little parlour, and quite another to
stand up, and with your own voice alone

to fill one hall as much bigger as your church as I am as you."

"But I do not want to stand up and sing in a large hall," I began.

"Then why did my good friend Dr. Packman say to me, 'When next you come down to catch our trouts, there is one——' "

A look from the Doctor arrested Herr Droigel at this point, and an awkward silence would have ensued but for Miss Packman, who said—

"I think what Annie wants is to take a few lessons here."

"A few lessons here!" repeated the Professor, lifting hands and eyes to heaven. "Mein Gott! what will she want next? and who is to give those few lessons? That clever man who taught her to play the piano perhaps—taught her so!" and he went to the instrument and mimicked my performance, while Dr. Packman shouted with laughter and I could have cried with rage.

" Or, perhaps," proceeded Herr Droigel,
" that skeleton woman you were so good
as to ask here once to spend one evening—
I remember her. I have not forgotten—
no ;" and he spread out his wide coat-tails,
curved his wrists well over the instrument,
and after sounding a few chords, touching
the notes as though they were hot, and
burnt him, he began in a falsetto, which
seemed doubly absurd emanating from such
a mountain of flesh, so admirable an imita-
tion of Madam Morrison's thready soprano,
that the tears I had been keeping back
on my own account, filled my eyes while
laughing at the ridicule thus cast on her.

It is not easy, we all know, to be perfectly good-humoured when a snowball,
judiciously aimed at the back of one's neck,
makes a channel for its trickling stream
between one's shoulder-blade and spinal
column. Nevertheless, with what equanimity, not to say pleasure, we behold another
bearing the same infliction.

"If not, then," suddenly resumed Herr Droigel, stopping his musical performances and taking up the argument after his German fashion precisely at the point where he had left it off—"if not, then, the clever pianist or the sylph-like madam, who remains to teach Miss Annie? Who is there to give those 'few lessons' your charming sister thinks it only needs to perfect the song of our young lady?"

"We will consider and talk over the matter," said the Doctor, in a curiously absent manner. "Meantime, what do you say to a cigar?"

"I say no," was the reply. "To a pipe among the roses, if Miss Packman thinks I can be of any service in killing her green flies, I say yes;" and accordingly they both produced their pipes, and walked into the garden, where I saw them smoking gravely and talking earnestly for a full hour, whilst Miss Packman industriously braided a velvet cap she meant to present to the Professor, and I grounded a pair of slippers it was her intention should at some future period adorn her brother's remarkably small feet.

According to our sexes, I consider we were all usefully and gracefully occupied.

When the gentlemen had finished their pipes and their conversation, it was time for me to tidily fold up my work and take my departure. Herr Droigel gallantly offered to see me safe across the green, and although I felt in his company like a cockle-shell boat in the wake of a seventy-four, still I was grateful to the large gentleman for his kindness, and tried to behave myself, as the nurses say, " prettily."

But he was in no mood for prettiness of behaviour. From some cause which I could not in the slightest degree under-stand, he seemed to be immensely in earnest, and the moment we were outside the gate, commenced impressing upon me the importance of playing no tricks with my voice.

"There is no one here who could teach you what would be good," he said; "and so our very good friend the Doctor and I have agreed you had better not learn at all. He tells me in his opinion you might be a degree stronger; do not sing much till you rise that degree; do not work too hard, you have years and years and years before you in which to work; but just now your first business is to be a little humming-bee, gathering honey, that is health. When you have laid in a good stock of that, then you shall sing; but do not sing, no not much now. You live, our dear Doctor says, with a grandmother—oh, so charming!— who loves you so much, whom you love so much. That is good; always love your grandmother. I had a grandmother once, whom I loved. I shall come and pay my respects to that delightful lady to-morrow, if she permit. Goot-night, Miss Annie. God bless you!" And he took my hand and held it in his immense palm a moment.

" God bless you !" he repeated, and dropped my hand ; and went away across the green, but not in the direction of the Doctor's house.

It is not an easy matter for any person, more especially for a young person, to repeat compliments that have, more or less judiciously, been paid during the course of an evening visit ; and therefore all I had to tell my grandmother seemed to please her well. Herr Droigel counselled my singing little, and having no lessons at all.

Hearing this she said—

" You are not disappointed, Annie ?"

" No," was my answer, "not at all." But like a little Jesuit I kept my reasons for not feeling disappointed to myself. Already I had learned the lesson that perfect frankness does not always add to the happiness and contentment of those with whom our lot is cast.

That night I slept in fairyland ; the dreams of my life became in sleep its realities ; and when I awoke they seemed almost realities still.

Bright grew my life, brighter and brighter as the weeks rolled on—for that dear Professor not merely threw out hints for my guidance while he stayed at Alford, but kept up a correspondence with me after his return to London, sending me now a few exercises written in the neatest of caligraphy, now a morsel of his own composition, sometimes a very simple song—"suited to my years and abilities"—more frequently a chant or hymn.

His letters were a delight to my grandmother. I am afraid he was a dreadful hypocrite, and wrote them with a view of pleasing her. He knew great people, and spoke of them and their doings with a covert satire which induced her to think— ah, how mistaken she was !—that he despised and disliked the fashionable world. He attended vast assemblies, and sent accounts of them to us more graphic than anything we ever read in the few papers that fell in our way.

And so the autumn passed, and winter came and went, and spring smiled on the earth once more, and summer was at hand again; and one Sunday evening, after we had returned from church (there was no chapel at Alford, and my grandmother, not being able to walk so far as formerly, and, farther, having made close acquaintance with the curate, had arrived at the conclusion that, so long as she heard the Gospel of Christ preached, it did not matter where she knelt in prayer), I sat at the piano, trying, before it passed out of my memory, to reproduce a new tune I had heard that night adapted to the words, "Nearer, my God, to Thee." After a short time I succeeded in picking out the melody, and then, improvising an accompaniment, I sang the hymn straight through.

"That is nice, grannie, is it not?" I said, when I ended.

She made no answer.

It was nothing unusual for her to fall asleep whilst I sang, so rising from the instrument, and walking quietly to one of the windows, I looked out across the green, which the moon was flooding with an almost unearthly light.

All at once the profound silence of the room struck me with a sort of horror, and hoping she would soon awaken, I turned towards the sleeper. Something in her attitude reminded me of that night when, coming from the Great House, I made up my mind I could never leave her.

Just as it had done then, her head leaned back against the chair, showing the thin worn cheeks, the lines of care, the marks traced by time and sorrow. Just as then, her hand hung over the arm listlessly, seeming almost powerless; but there was something more than this, or else the pale moonbeams falling across her face deceived me—something I had never seen before in any face.

"Grannie!" I said.

There came no reply.

"Grannie!" I repeated louder.

She would not waken. In an access of terror I threw my arms around her, but there was no answering caress.

What happened next? When help came, I found myself standing in the middle of the carpet with the bell-rope in my hand.

After that there was an interval, when I felt as though I had fallen down a cliff and stunned myself, and was slowly recovering my senses. Then I heard people talking, and have a faint memory of being led out of the room and the house ; of passionately resisting the strength of some one stronger than I ; of being compelled to swallow something ; of sinking into a deep sleep, and waking up suddenly with a pang, in a strange bed in a strange house ; of crying out, "Where am I ? Where am I ? What has happened?" of hearing a voice broken by sobs answer, "Oh, my dear !" and then I understood.

I gave no one any trouble after that ; I turned my face to the wall, comprehending what had come to pass ; and though IT was in another house, I lay alone till morning with my dead.

CHAPTER IV.

MY BEREAVEMENT.

NO matter how much people may differ in temperament and constitution, there is, I fancy, a wonderful similarity in the manner in which they spend the first twenty-four hours after some one near and dear has been taken from them.

Of course there are deaths and deaths. The miser crawls unwillingly from out his money-bags, and quits a world he has helped to cumber, leaving no one to lament his departure. The prodigal who comes after him dies; and his boon companions flee from the sight of a fate they would fain forget overtakes all who are born of woman. There is the death waited for by paid nurses, certified by the regular medical attendant, announced to the world generally in the obituary column, and to passers-by particularly, by closely-drawn blinds. There is the long-expected death, which has not come by years so soon as it might; when the dinner-bell rings just the same as usual, and the inhabitants of the mansion eat and drink, and talk, and sleep, as they did before; for the actual death which has come seems to them almost less terrible than the mockery of life, that for so long fought in a lonely upper chamber to preserve its own wretched existence. There are deaths which, even in the first hours that follow, survivors cannot regard other than as a relief and a blessing.

But these are the exceptions; taking it as a rule, death deals a very hard blow to the survivors. They may recover from it soon, or bear traces of it to their graves; they may weep over their loss passionately, or go about the usual affairs of life with dry eyes and stern set faces; or they may wrap themselves up in a wordless anguish, to which God in His own good time alone can bring comfort. Still, with all these differences, no matter how the rue may be worn, the experience of the first twenty-four hours is the same to most people.

There is the shock of bereavement; whether sudden or long expected, matters less than is generally supposed; whether it comes " so soon" or " at last" makes little or no difference in the mystery at length revealed. To that shock follows the numbed incredulity of non-comprehension, a stupid, stubborn refusal to believe the worst, and then forgetfulness brought on by physical and mental exhaustion; to which, in due time, succeeds the worst trial of all—the waking to daylight, to memory, to sorrow.

One gone who may never return; one set sail across that ocean, the tide whereof is always ebbing, never flowing; one departed from the old home, who may not re-enter its portals; one less in the world, who was all the world to some loving heart ; one passed forth solitary on the dark lonely journey ; a voice silenced, eyes closed, heart stilled, pulses quiet.

And the birds sing, and the sun shines, and the flowers bloom, and the leaves dance in the morning breeze ; and the mourner rises to look forth upon the earth, which can never again seem quite the same earth as it did before the curse was thus made visible.

It had come. That wolf, whose gaunt wicked apparition I conjured up one morning in the old garden at Lovedale, had come when I least expected to see him, when nothing was farther from my thoughts than sorrow, or sickness, or death, and carried off all I loved in the world, all I had in the world to love me.

When I woke from the sleep which towards morning visited me, I felt like a bankrupt in earthly hope and earthly affection. She was gone—no family Bible, no moss-grown tombstone, no average of three-score-and-ten or three-score-and-anything could give me comfort again ; one moment she was with me, the next she had departed.

In an early chapter I said I tried her as a duckling might a hen, and she tried me as a hen might a duckling ; nevertheless, the hen supplies a mother's place to the duckling, and grannie, dear dead grannie, had supplied that place to me.

I dressed myself in haste. Mine was a terrible face to see, as I caught sight of it in the glass, and I shrunk from its reflection as one instinctively retreats from something painful and unlovely—dishevelled hair, cheeks pale, with a crimson spot on the top of each, eyes sunken with weeping, lids swollen from the same cause; a contrast, I wot, to the white quiet face lying up-turned in our cottage, that I meant never to leave more till the coffin-lid closed over it.

Like one committing a crime, I stole from the house of those friends who had—

meaning to be very kind—brought me away from her.

Not to seem ungrateful, I left a line on the dressing-table—telling them I must "go back to grannie" was, I have since understood, the formula used—and this done I made my way into the open air, and speeding across the village green, soon reached our cottage, where Jack was milking Cowslip as if nothing special had occurred, and Jill was sitting before a newly-kindled fire in the kitchen, weeping fit to break her heart, with her apron thrown over her head.

"Betty"—that was the name of the then Jill of our establishment—"Oh, Betty!" I said ; and then we sat down hand in hand, and cried together. Jill had lost a kind mistress, and I the only mother I could remember.

Dr. Packman and his sister were very good to me at this juncture ; they let me remain with the dead ; and although Miss Packman spent most part of the days which succeeded at the cottage, she did not insist on bringing her bag and baggage also, and cumbering me and Jill in the first access of our grief with a visitor.

Betty and I had much of each other's company at that crisis, and were the better for it. She brought a mattress into my room and slept there, and was ready with her tears when she heard me sobbing in the night.

There was no bitterness about my grief. If I had not done all for the dead that I might—and whose actions will in his own sight bear weighing in the scales at that supreme moment?—at all events I had been a comfort to grannie, and she loved me. The time spent at Alford had been a season of uninterrupted peace and happiness—at least, so it seemed to me; but I did not know, as I lay awake at night thinking over it all, that it had not been all happiness to her.

We none of us thoroughly understand

the other. I comprehended later that she had kept all trouble from me so long as she could.

Sooner than I could have supposed it possible for him to arrive, my uncle Isaac knocked at the door, which I opened for him.

He was dressed all in black, and had precisely that look in his face which a man usually wears when, full of trouble himself, he thinks he will be called upon to comfort the trouble of others as well.

I do not know in what state he expected to find me, but he must have felt relieved at my meeting him; for his eyes brightened in an instant, and the hard set expression about his mouth relaxed as he took my hand in his, and said only two words—

" Nannie, dear !"

That was all. I never spoke; I could not speak. We went into the parlour together, and for full five minutes, I should say, he stood beside the window, although the blind was drawn down; his hands plunged deep in his pockets, his eyes fixed on the carpet, silent as I was myself.

At the end of that time, which seemed like an hour to me, he turned and said—

" Where is she ? You needn't come, only tell me." I had not far to take him, only across the hall; for in our little drawing-room, where she died, they had laid her down in that sleep which might never on earth be broken. The furniture was arranged formally against the walls, the piano was closed, the ornaments piled up on a table in one corner, while in the centre were placed tressels, which supported a shell containing that he desired to see.

He entered, and I, closing the door, left the middle-aged man with his mother.

He stayed a long while with her. Who can tell what memories he recalled, what deeds he wished undone, what hours he would have given years of his existence to live over again, what prayers he uttered, what vows he made—alone then with God and the dead! I only know that when at length he joined me, his face was very white, and its expression sadder and sterner than any I had ever seen there before.

"Will you come out with me?" he asked; and I put on a bonnet and scarf, and we went away together into the cool dark woods, where the brook went trickling over the pebbles and gravel, making a music like that of distant faëry bells.

"You have lost your best friend, Nannie," he began, after we had walked for some time in silence; "and I have lost mine. We must try to be good friends to one another."

I could not answer him. His speech made my comprehension of the utter desolation that had come upon me, more vivid even than before.

"It was not unexpected to her," he went on. "Before I came to see you at Christmas, I knew that sooner or later I should receive just such a message as Dr. Packman sent me on Monday. I had a letter from her so long back as last summer, which I brought over for you to read. If it would grieve you to look at it now——"

"No," I interrupted, stretching out my hand to take the familiar writing ; "only first tell me why, if—if you knew, she kept it——"

"Why she did not confide in you as well?" he finished. "For this reason, dear : she did not wish your feet to be set in the Valley of the Shadow one hour before it was actually necessary."

"But I should like to have known," I said. "Oh, grannie, if you had only told me !"—and the tears so long repressed burst their bounds as I thought of all the hours I might have spent with her,

of all I might have done for her, had I
ever guessed there was danger approach-
ing.

He let me cry for a space. He sat silent
beside the stream, while I—hands flung
wildly forward, face buried in the cool
moss—sobbed as though my heart were
breaking.

"If you had been expecting this daily
for a year," he said at last, speaking slowly
and gently, "it would not have seemed one
bit the less hard now. You were too
young, Nannie, to have borne such knowledge, as we older people are forced to
do, patiently. Life would have stood still
for you in the expectation of death; ordinary duties would have been cast aside;
the laughter my mother loved to hear
would have echoed no longer; the step
she liked to watch, so light and quick,
would have grown slow and thoughtful;
your pleasant talk would have had a con-
straint upon it; and instead of the memory

of a year of happiness, you would now be looking back upon twelve months clouded by the anticipation of a trouble which was incapable of being averted by you or any other human being."

"But, oh, uncle, if I had only known!" I repeated, my face still buried in the moss, now wet with scalding tears.

"What could you have done, dear?"

Ay, that was the question—what could I have done—I, so feeble, so powerless, though I loved her so much?

"Do you suppose, if any means had seemed likely to avail, I should have left those means untried?"

"No," I murmured.

"Then why should you wish to have known when you could have done nothing for her?"

I lifted up my face from the ground, and pushed back the hair that had fallen in tangled masses over my forehead. I could answer him now, for the vague

impressions left by his first announcement
had taken a definite shape at last.

"If I had a great trouble," I replied,
"I should not like to bear it all alone, even
if no one could help me."

The stream rippled on at our feet, the
birds' songs sounded overhead; there ensued a pause, during which I could hear
the melody of the stream, the chorus
of the birds. Then my companion said
softly—

"When you have such a trouble as
this, or a trouble greater, if that be possible, I trust that ONE, nearer and dearer
even than little Annie was to her grandmother, will help you to bear it."

And he took off his hat when he spoke,
as though he had been in church.

It was an incongruous idea, and I hated
my imagination for harbouring it at such
a moment; but I could not help wondering
how a man like this had ever brought himself to marry his wife.

True, Mrs. Isaac Motfield was not unaccustomed to religious musings and observations, but her remarks usually tended to the conclusion that the special Providence which directed the concerns of her and hers had either no time or no inclination to consider the affairs of other people.

Never, save in the cant of some utterly hypocritical time-server, did religion present a more repulsive aspect than when portrayed by the word-painting of Mrs. Isaac Motfield. Vaguely, spite of my sorrow, the memory of some of the sentences I had heard that woman utter would recur to my mind, and at the same moment a question, which never ceased to trouble me for very long at a time, once again presented itself; and in order to have it solved, I asked—

" Where, uncle, will — the ——"

" I suppose you mean, dear, where shall we bury her ?" he said, as I stopped, not liking to pronounce the word. " If you read the letter I gave you, and I think it may be well for you to do so, that will tell you all."

Saying which he rose and left me, while I perused that message from the dead.

At first the writing seemed dim and indistinct, by reason of the tears which welled up in my eyes and blinded me ; but by degrees that control, learned in the calm unimpassioned school wherein all the lessons of my life had been conned, asserted itself, and I read her words, as I would have tried to listen to them if spoken on her death-bed, quietly.

After some commonplace sentences, touching a pecuniary remittance, domestic matters, and the health of her daughter-in-law and grandchildren, the letter proceeded :—

" Now, my dear son, I have some bad news to tell, which I think it only right you should know. I have not, as I told you in my last, felt very well for some time, and so I determined to consult a medical man. He tells me—for I begged him to keep nothing back—that my heart is seriously affected, and that the mischief has been going on for years. I thank God for giving me so many free from ache or pain, or knowledge of coming illness! Leading the quiet regular life I do, free from care, it is possible and probable, he says, that following certain rules, my life may be prolonged for a considerable time longer; on the other hand, a day, an hour, a minute may end it.

" At first this seemed to me very terrible; but when I come to think it over, what more has the doctor said to me now than I have heard repeated every Sunday since I first went to the little chapel in Love-dale ?

" My days are not yet numbered, though one day more may find my place vacant; but the uncertainty of life, so far as I am concerned, has been put before me in a way I can never forget; and for this reason I want to put my house in order, so that when the hour strikes no worldly concerns may trouble me.

"As soon as may be convenient, I should like you to come over, that I may tell you exactly what I have done ; only remember, Annie must know nothing of all this. Trouble will come upon her soon enough without our making it for her. She has been the blessing of my old age, the light and life of a home which, but for her, must indeed have seemed dark and lonely.

"I do not want her to shed a tear for me before the time actually comes. I want to see the sunshine on her young face until night closes over me. Isaac, you will be a father to that dear child. I don't dictate where she shall live, what you shall do with her little money, how her education shall go on. I leave you her guardian—I leave her present and her future to God.

"If I did not believe He would keep her from all harm I should fear sometimes for her happiness ; and yet every day I feel more and more assured that, although her ways are not my ways, she will be kept from the evil, if not from trouble. The lady whose school she attends called here yesterday, and told me that if Annie ever should require to take a situation, she would be most happy to engage her as a junior teacher. This is an unspeakable relief to me, as it would at once give the poor dear a home and a chance of cheaply finishing her education.

"Every one seems to like the child, though she is so shy before strangers. I pray she may always make good friends— I mean friends who will teach her nothing but what is right.

"My dear son, this is a long letter for me to write. I have been two days about it already, and have not yet finished.

"There are one or two things I still want to say : *whenever* I go and *wherever*, lay my body in the graveyard most convenient at the time.

" You recollect when I left Lovedale my saying foolishly I should like to be buried beside your father. I have learned better since. He will be as near me if I rest under the turf here as if you put us side by side.

" Concerning the little I have to leave, Annie has no part in it save in my love and gratitude. My own children are nearest in blood. Amongst them I have equally divided all the worldly goods I own, but I desire you to see that the money which came to Annie from her father is touched by no one save for her benefit ; and I wish you to understand I have left a list of all the articles in the cottage which are her property, and oh, my son, be kind to this the only orphan we have in the family—in proportion to the charge shall be the reward. Some may, perhaps, think I have loved the child too much, but if you hear this said, remember all she has been to me.

" Certainly I can declare since she was

first put in my arms she has never wilfully caused me an anxious hour. If she is different from us all, the Almighty made her so. You first pointed this out to me. Remember *that* night, Isaac, when I am here no longer."

There was more than this, more added at later dates, for the letter occupied a week in writing; but I could read no farther then.

What had I lost? what had I not lost? In a great hurry, with a terrible tremor, I went in search of my uncle, whom I discovered not far distant.

"Let us go home," I said; "let us go home, please, now."

"Why home, Nannie?" he asked.

"Because I want to be near her as long as I can," was my reply.

"But you trust me, dear, don't you?" he asked. "I will be all to you she asks, and more."

By way of answer, I put my arms round

his neck and kissed him, as I apprehend no child of his own had ever done before.

Then, hand clasped in hand, we retraced our steps, through the woods, across the green, to the silent darkened dwelling where she lay so still and quiet.

CHAPTER V.

CONCERNING MY FUTURE.

THE next morning brought an influx of Motfields and other relations to that once peaceful home. People I had never seen before took possession of the house as though it belonged to them of right. People I had only vaguely heard of, asked if I was "that girl," and receiving an answer in the affirmative, shook their heads in grave disapproval of my existence and myself.

Mrs. Daniel Motfield was there, but Mrs. Isaac, having it in contemplation about that period to increase the population of Fairport, put in no appearance—to my exceeding comfort, be it confessed.

Before the arrival of this goodly company, my Uncle Isaac, assisted by Dr. Packman, occupied himself in putting away all plate, nicknacks, ornaments, papers, articles of wearing apparel, and so forth, in boxes, cupboards, and drawers, whereto seals were at once attached. Nothing moveable, indeed, was left, save the general furniture, of which they took an inventory, and my own wearing apparel, which no one considered sufficiently valuable to put under lock and key.

"Nannie," said my uncle to me on the morning of *that* day, "you had better go over this morning to Miss Packman; she will be glad to have you."

"Let me stay," I answered; "I will stop in my own room."

And he humoured me. Amongst that throng I had no desire to follow my dead —mine if theirs; and when they had all departed, the silent house, the stillness broken by no sound save that of the tolling bell, was more eloquent to me of one "gone before" than the dark procession, the gaping grave.

When it was all over, when earth had been given to earth, and dust returned to dust, when the mourners had come back, and cake and wine had duly been eaten and drunk, Dr. Packman knocked at my door.

"Miss Annie," he said, "as a matter of form you had better come downstairs; the will is going to be read."

"What have I to do with her will?" I asked.

"Happily, nothing," he answered; "nevertheless, do as I tell you;" and I obeyed.

How the men and the women assembled below scowled at me as, holding Dr. Packman's hand, I entered! They edged closer together, moving away from the corner we occupied, as though I had brought contagion into the room.

"Shouldn't wonder if she has left the girl every farthing," I heard one very evil-looking man remark, after which there was a "hush-sh!" and the attorney, who had nodded to me pleasantly and encouragingly, began.

The will was very short. She had been possessed of little, and at her death she divided it fairly and simply amongst all her "dear children." To her grandchild, Annie Trenet, being already provided for, she left merely her love and blessing. She appointed her eldest son Isaac guardian of the said Annie Trenet, and named Isaac Motfield and Dr. Decimus Packman executors.

"That is all, ladies and gentlemen," said the lawyer, when he finished reading, marvelling apparently at the dead hush and silence which succeeded ; and he rose, and will in hand stood, so it seemed to me, inviting comment.

There ensued a pause, which was broken at length by the husband of some one of my unknown aunts.

"I call that a will such as all wills should be," he said, in an accent which actually

appalled me. "And what I mean to say is
this : we have all done Miss Annie there a
great injustice, and I for one am sorry for
it. Will you shake hands, niece ?"

Thus accosted, what could I do but
comply with his request, having the pleasure
at the same time of hearing Mrs. Daniel
Motfield remark—

"Artful little baggage ! she has been
living on the fat of the land all these years
past."

"Artful baggage yourself, ma'am, or
civil language, if *you* please," shouted my
latest champion, who, I discovered subsequently, had married a female Motfield
older even than my Uncle Isaac. "I say
the will is a just will; and more nor that,
I say, if ever this young lady wants a friend,
I'll stand by her. Now, my dear, maybe
you'll want a home."

"No," interrupted Dr. Packman, decidedly ; "not while my sister and I have
one to offer her. But Miss Annie has

money. Her future residence must be decided by her sole guardian;" and he indicated Uncle Isaac.

"Oh, we understand all about that. He has played his cards well," said Mrs. Daniel, who was simply irrepressible, as I knew to my cost.

At this juncture I got up; I did not care for Mrs. Daniel or the whole assembled multitude.

"Take me from them, uncle," I cried, crossing the room to where he stood. "Take me away anywhere; there is not one of them who loved grannie one bit."

It was an accusation they could not answer. They made way for us to pass without a word more being spoken, and you, and you, and you, who have lived in the world, and understand its pleasant ways, can guess how my relatives loved me after that confession of faith.

What did their love or hate matter to me, however? She, the only woman excepting my mother who had ever cared for me, was dead; what farther sorrow could time or experience bring?

That was what youth said; what time and experience said is quite another affair.

Then I had but youth to consult, and that which youth bid me do I did. For hours at a stretch I sat in the churchyard, beside a grave my own hands had beautified; I wept in passionate despair when I woke in the mornings, I cried through the day, I sobbed myself to sleep at night.

In the presence of others I kept my grief in the background, and fancied no one suspected how much I fretted, but in this I was wrong. It had been tacitly agreed amongst those who at that time interested themselves about my welfare, it was best the fever of trouble should be left to take its own course; and when I came to my senses again, it filled me with a terrible feeling of shame to find how, while I fancied I was bearing my sorrow silently and alone, every one had been really studying my wishes, humouring my whims, keeping silence at times when speech would have proved far easier, if not one-half so wise.

When many weeks had passed, when the first grief was spent, when I had begun dimly to understand that the affairs of life must go on, whether people were happy or miserable, my Uncle Isaac came over to Alford once again.

By advice of Dr. Packman, my fancy for remaining in the cottage had hitherto been indulged.

True, they did not leave me alone there all day, but they left me sufficiently alone to humour the idea that no one ever tried to come between me and my grief. Now, however, it was necessary to consider the future. Where was I to live? with whom, and how?

If the cottage were let, it was estimated a sufficient annual income could be secured to enable me to reside with some quiet family, and to continue my studies. Dr. Packman and his sister wished to give me a home free of all charge, but to this arrangement my uncle would by no means consent.

"Nannie cannot intrude on the kindness of friends for ever," he said; "and what she is to do, and what she is to be, had better be decided now than hereafter."

"Herr Droigel will be with us the day after to-morrow," suggested Dr. Packman; "would it not be well to defer coming to any conclusion until we hear his opinion?"

"What has Herr Droigel to do with the matter?" inquired my uncle.

"Ask your niece," replied the Doctor, looking significantly at me.

But I exclaimed—

"No, no; I shall never sing—I shall never want to sing again."

"Time will do wonders for you, my dear," said the Doctor, kindly; while my uncle, without taking any notice of my declaration, remarked—

"I thought Herr Droigel said it would be better for her not to sing much, not to take singing lessons at all."

"He did say so," was the answer, "but there was a reason for that, which I will explain presently. Meantime, before opening any communication with Mrs. Mitchell concerning the pupil-teacher plan, to which it is evident you incline, I should like you to have ten minutes' chat with Droigel."

"We need not wait for Herr Droigel, Doctor," I interrupted, petulantly; "I shall never sing again."

"Very well, dear," said Dr. Packman. "No one shall force you into any course distasteful to your feelings; nevertheless," he added, *sotto voce*, "we will wait for my friend."

After that conversation I had a relapse into despair. The mere mention of my voice brought back all the anxiety it had caused, all the changes it had wrought. Over and over again I repeated to myself the words I spoke to Dr. Packman—" Nothing should ever induce me to sing ; I would never open a piano more." Sitting in the graveyard, under the shade of an ancient yew-tree, which sheltered the spot where she lay, I tormented myself by wishing that my grandmother could only understand how completely in unison our ideas on that vexed question were at last.

I was there in the quiet hush of a summer's afternoon, quite alone. My uncle had gone with Dr. Packman for a drive, and it was arranged that on the morrow Herr Droigel's opinion as to my future career should be taken.

To rebel against that opinion was my firm intention. Now she was dead, I resolved never to adopt a profession my grandmother would have disapproved of my entering during her life-time.

I made that resolution beside her grave,

and offered it to her memory, just in the same spirit as I had gathered flowers, and laid them on the turf that covered her resting-place. How calm and peaceful and still everything seemed! The gardens of Little Alford Manor-house, that sloped down quite to the wall of the churchyard, the woods beyond with scarce a breath of air stirring the leaves, the quiet graveyard with its many grassy hillocks, its few and simple headstones, the old, old church, with its small diamond-paned windows, its low tower covered to the very top with ivy, its grey weather-beaten walls, its tiled roof, and its lych-gate. There was not a creature moving, not a human being crossed, while I remained, the footpath that led away first to the meadows, where cows chewed the cud lazily, and farther on to a stream, where under the alders the speckled trout flashed in and out of deep clear silent pools.

Everything in the landscape was peaceful

and beautiful. I alone felt at discord with Nature. Firmly I then believed the sight of the sun would never bring happiness to me again. What good I proposed to myself or the dead by sitting thus, I cannot imagine. I only know I stayed till the shadow thrown by the church-tower warned me it was time to return to our cottage. Rising slowly from the ground, I was about to leave the place, when a voice close at hand said softly—

"Soh, my poor little maiden, it is thus we meet once more;" and Herr Droigel, for it was he, took my hand in both of his, while he shook his great head mournfully, with an expression of tender sentiment, that would at any other time have seemed to me irresistibly funny, pervading his fat face.

"You have suffered," he went on, "that is bad; you eat nothing, you sleep little, that is worse; you sit here thinking to bring back your dead to life, that is worst of all. My little child, did I not tell thee

it was good for you to love your grandmother? Yes. Then I tell thee now it is
good for you to leave her. She would tell
you this if that tongue so silent could speak.
She would say, ' Mine love, weeping beside
my grave is not what you should be doing.'
She would say, ' Have pity on your pretty
buds, and make up no garlands to wither
in memoriam of one whose eyes now behold
the flowers of Paradise.' She would say,
' You have shed many, many tears; shed
no more, because I am where there are no
tears.' She would say, ' There is a time
for weeping and a time for rejoicing; you
have wept; you should now rejoice, because
there are so many good kind friends left
who love you much.' Come;" and he drew
my hand within his arm, and thus we
walked together to Dr. Packman's house.

Arrived there, we found tea ready, and
Miss Packman, her brother, and my uncle
in the drawing-room.

" And now, good gentlemen both," said

Herr Droigel, when, after seeing me comfortably seated, he drew up a chair to the table preparatory to commencing an attack on the good things Miss Packman had provided for him—" and now, good gentlemen both, you remember when I went out I said I would give you one reply when I came back. My reply is—I make no advice about Miss Annie except Miss Annie's self be close at my elbow to hear.

" Miss Annie being here, when I have eaten, when I have drunken some cups of amiable Miss Packman's tea, we will talk. Eat, mine love," he went on, addressing me ; " you will never understand our talk, if you listen to it while starving."

There was no fear of Herr Droigel failing to understand the conversation if quantities of food were stimulants to comprehension.

Before his gigantic appetite disappeared mountains of bread-and-butter, hillocks of toasted cakes, a dish covered with slices of ham, and the best part of a cold fowl. To this succeeded a second course of jellies, jams, and marmalade; and when he had finished that, and half a dozen large cups of tea, he wound up with about a quart of strawberries, which he literally drowned in cream, in turn solidifying the cream with half a basinful of powdered white sugar.

When he had demolished this last enemy he heaved a sigh, complimented Miss Packman on "her delicate consideration in remembering the preferences of her devoted Droigel," pushed his chair back, and inquired if what we had to say could not be talked over amongst the "roses and the lilies."

Without doubt it is this "roses and lilies" business which makes those who have been thrown much in contact with Germans so bitter against and so suspicious of those of the Fatherland who honour our country with their presence. When a man finds that all this charm of manner covers something which is not in the least charming in its results; when he discovers that underneath the velvet glove lurks the grasp of iron ; that subservient to all other human interests lies the desire of self-aggrandizement, it becomes very difficult to tolerate figures of speech and graces of sentiment.

" Your money or your life," may not be a pleasant form of words, but it possesses at least the advantage of perfect intelligibility.

When precisely the same result has been compassed by a more gracefully-turned sentence, or series of sentences, the deceitfulness of the procedure only aggravates the rage of the victim.

We, sitting among the roses and lilies of Herr Droigel's sentiment, were, however, novices to all this sort of thing, and listened to the graces of language to which Herr Droigel treated us in the same frame of mind as that with which one might contemplate the antics of a kitten.

With what delight, by the way, must these foreigners observe the tolerant self-complacency wherewith English people regard them !

If we could catch a glimpse of them, when the mask is off, the disguise of that " so charming simplicity " put on one side, as a man might don a useful topcoat, should we not find these " mere children of nature" screaming with laughter and exclaiming in their detestable gutturals—

" What a fool is this dear John Bull, what a fool is Mrs. Bull, what fools are the young ladies and the young gentlemen, sons and daughters of John and his wife !"

As before indicated, however, we listened to Herr Droigel that evening even as he himself would have tenderly put it, " like calves of the Bull family ;" thereby implying a more touching extent of gullibility than is to be found ordinarily amongst that bucolic race.

Certainly we knew no more of Germany, of the cleverness of its inhabitants, of the dexterity with which they can manipulate conversation and blow bubbles in the air all the time they are really trying to catch fish in the stream, than the babes in the wood.

Happy was it for us, simpletons as we were, that Herr Droigel was so honest a rogue, so clever a self-seeker, so straightforward a deceiver, so virtuous a hypocrite as time proved him to be.

Had he been treacherous as Delilah we should have fallen into his hands all the same.

" Sit here, Miss Annie," began the large creature, grouping us to his satisfaction on some seats placed under a mulberry-tree in the Doctor's old-fashioned garden, " you and I are old friends ; we understand one another. Come and sit near to your own Droigel, who has been put on the rack, who has been subjected to what your merciful lawgivers used to call the question, all for you. Yes, it is true ; no sooner did I arrive here this afternoon, seeking rest and repose after the heat and burden, than Miss Packman commences to speak about 'Annie,' whom she loves as her own sister. She has not finished talking before two gentlemen appear in a gig. They are both hot, having of their own free will been driving in the sun, but they are not so hot as their horse, which, without any will of its own, has been driven in the sun—poor horse!

" One of these pair says, pointing to the other, ' This is Annie's uncle, Mr. Motfield— my old and valued friend Herr Droigel.'

" Droigel stands two inches higher in his shoes, and is charmed.

" Then Dr. Packman says, ' It is desirable some decision should be come to concerning Annie's future ;' and Mr. Motfield adds, ' What should you advise, Herr Droigel ?' And how do you suppose I answered your friends, Miss Annie ?" finished Herr Droigel, turning suddenly towards me.

"I fancy you did not answer them at all," I said, remembering his speech made before he had, to quote his own phrase, "eaten and drunken."

"Wrong, Miss Annie," was his reply. "I answered, 'I am going out, gentlemen, for a few minutes; when I return I shall have pleasure to reply to you.'"

Then ensued a silence, which no one else seeming disposed to break, Herr Droigel again took up his parable—

"I went across the green common to the pretty house I remembered; there was no Annie there. I asked a servant, not pretty, but good—good I should say certainly—where I might find the young miss, and the servant pointed a finger towards the church-tower. So I went softly to God's-acre, with a light tread and a heavy heart, and there I found this child sitting beside a grave, on which newly-woven wreaths were already withering. I brought her back with me. That is my little story ; suppose, gentlemen, you now tell yours."

Once again there ensued a pause, which was broken, however, this time by Dr. Packman—

"When you were here last summer Annie sang for you, and you said she had a voice."

"Mein Gott! I only hope she has not lost it," ejaculated Herr Droigel ; "but eating nothing, drinking nothing, crying much, sitting in damp graveyards—that is not the way to preserve a voice. No doubt," he added, mournfully, "the gift has been withdrawn, the lute broken. I warned you that organ was delicate. Do not blame me if the life in it has been destroyed."

"But, my good friend, you said to me yourself——" began Dr. Packman, excitedly.

"But, mein goot friend, you said to me yourself," interrupted Herr Droigel, with imperturbable calmness—"come nearer to me, Miss Annie, and you shall hear just what he said. Here where we sit, while we two were smoking our pipes, I asked, 'What does all this mean—what is the mystery?' and then he began : 'Droigel, the girl must not go to London yet. She is an orphan ; she has always lived with a grandmother, and they are devoted to each other. The old lady's time here cannot be long. That is the meaning and the mystery.' So now, Miss Annie, you know why I told you to get strong and love your grandmother. Complete frankness is best ; I love not secrets and reserves and whispers."

" It seems to me," interposed my uncle, " that the future and the present are what we are now concerned with. The past signifies little."

" It signifies a great deal," exclaimed Herr Droigel, with emotion. " Himmel ! to think of a whole year having been lost at her age ; and yet not lost," he added, remembering his former sentiments—" not lost, since it was spent with one this dear Miss Annie loved so much."

And he took my hand and stroked it reflectively.

" Well, the past cannot be recalled, at all events," said Dr. Packman. " Mr. Motfield is quite right there ; and what we have now to decide is, whether Annie shall go to Mrs. Mitchell's as a pupil-teacher, or——"

" What is a pupil-teacher ?" interrupted the German ; and on being informed he remarked, " Proceed. I beg your pardon for being so rude as to break in on your sentence, only I want to make my points as we go on."

" Or," continued Dr. Packman, "whether she shall devote herself to the musical profession."

" Meaning——" suggested Herr Droigel.

" Meaning, in other words," explained Dr. Packman, " shall she be a governess or a singer ?"

" Good ; that is, supposing she has not lost her voice, and can sing," observed Herr Droigel. " And now what says Miss Annie herself?"

" I shall never sing again."

" Good, once more. Now, gentlemen both, have you said your says ? Have you, Miss Annie, said your little say ?"

" I believe so," answered my uncle, while Doctor Packman nodded ; and I repeated my statement in a different form, " I shall be a governess ;" of which statement Herr Droigel did not take any notice beyond stroking my hand solemnly and thoughtfully once more.

" You English have a charming adage about buying a pig in a poke. I do not know what a poke is—I never met anybody who did ; but I take it to mean that no one but a fool plays at cards blindfold. You have done me so great honour as to ask my advice about this dear Miss Annie. If I ask two three questions you will not

say, when my broad back is turned, That
Droigel, what a most horribly rude fellow
he is ! prying into this thing, peering into
that."

"Ask any questions you like," said my
uncle, heartily. "I think we have all the
same object at heart."

Quite true, dear uncle ; the same object,
with a difference, happily, perhaps for me.

"Very good; I thank you, Mr. Motfield.
Now you and Dr. Packman, my highly-
esteemed old friend, seem agreed that as
a matter of living—bread-and-butter, we
shall say—it is necessary this young miss
should turn her attention to teaching other
young misses.   That is so ?"

"That is so," answered my uncle.

"And why is it so ?—forgive me if I
seem rude beyond imagination.   Regard
me as a doctor; this good child is sick ;
I want to know what prescription to make,
I ask questions that seem to you babble."

"The greater part of my mother's income

died with her," was the reply, "and the part which did not she divided equally amongst her children, purposely excluding Annie from all interest in it."

"What had Miss Annie done?"

"She had money of her own—more, by far, than my mother could give to her children. I think the will a just one; there should be no favouritism in families."

"Then Miss Annie is in a small way an heiress, as our good friend here gave me to understand?"

"Yes, but only in a small way. She would have enough—if the cottage could be let advantageously—to live on had she been different—of a different nature, I mean."

"I understand; it is the *noblesse oblige* element which causes difficulty. Miss Annie is a young lady, and has been brought up as a young lady should be. And you think, my dear," this to me, "it will please you to be a governess?"

"I think I must be one," I answered. "By my own wish money has been spent on my education; it would never do to have that money wasted."

"And how much, if I may inquire, has been spent upon this learning?" asked Herr Droigel.

"Books, and everything included, about a hundred pounds," answered my uncle.

"Gott in Himmel!" ejaculated Herr Droigel, "and nothing for it, nothing!"

"I dined at Mrs. Mitchell's every day," I explained.

"Dined, yes, that is something. At the quality of the dinner I make no guess. What knowledge you got might not fill that;" and he touched the bowl of his pipe significantly.

"Mrs. Mitchell would give me a small salary even now," I said, with a sense of offended dignity pervading my manner.

"Are you quite sure of that, my dear?" he asked, then continued. "No doubt,

though, she would give you a premium to
teach other young misses to know as little
as you do. Yes, dat is England," and he
looked on the ground, in deep thought,
whilst I, swelling with anger, was compelled to keep silence, because I really did
not know in what form of words to express
my feelings.

"I am of opinion that Miss Annie and
the respectable Mrs. Mitchell would get
on most admirably together," said Herr
Droigel at length; " but still if I was you and
Miss Annie, I would think over that matter
for a week. As Miss Annie has made up
her mind so certainly never to sing more,
it is of no use inquiring whether her voice
is gone or not."

After which Herr Droigel devoted himself to an admiring contemplation of the
roses and lilies. I do not think I ever
hated a human being as I detested the fat
German, the while I watched his ponderous
figure stooping over the flowers, caressing

with his great hands "the dear buds," so he styled them.

I did not then understand the real cause of my mortification and disgust, but I comprehend now it is one thing to say we will never use a talent again, but quite another not to be asked to exercise it.

Only the other afternoon Herr Droigel told me, in an unwonted burst of confidence, that he understood the "little ways of womans."

If he ever reads these pages he can take the satisfaction out of them of knowing I thoroughly believe *that* statement, at all events.

CHAPTER VI.

WE ARE ALL SATISFIED.

EFORE we had finished breakfast next morning Herr Droigel entered the room.

"I have come to make one request," he said to my uncle. "Whilst Miss Annie is attending to her little household cares, following the example of Desdemona the bewitching, will you walk with me? Our good friend Packman is, as usual, off to see patients and make fees—what a charming profession is that of a doctor!—and that adorable Miss Packman, whom I have lofed ever since mine eyes first rested on her countenance, is engaged also, as becomes an English lady, in various works of domestic use. It is a heavenly morning. Say, dear sir, will the sun and the sky tempt you ?"

"The sun and the sky might not," answered my uncle, "but you, Herr Droigel, are irresistible."

Whereupon the German laid his hand on his waistcoat and bowed, with that utter oblivion of the possibility of there being anything ridiculous in his appearance, which is usual amongst foreigners.

"And how is Miss Annie to-day ?" he went on. "To my thinking a little *triste*— a trifle what you call out of sorts."

"I am not out of sorts," I answered ; "I am only tired."

"Tired ; that is bad," he said, with such an expression of sudden and genuine concern in his face, that I felt more than half inclined to condone his offences of omission and commission. "I do not like to hear a young miss say she is tired so early that she can have had no time to get weary. If you were my child, I should carry you off

from Alford. I would let your eyes look on
the Rhine. If you could not walk, I would
carry you up the Swiss mountains. You
should loiter at Geneva, and take Paris on
your way home. No more 'tiredness'
then. You would be your old self, the Miss
Annie I made friends with twelve months
ago."

"I am certain a change would do her a
world of good," agreed my uncle.

"Good! yes, I should think it would.
Before she goes to Madam Mitchell, she
ought to have one, two, three months' holi-
day. Yes, Miss Annie, I am right. You
have been weeping; you have been sitting
beside damp graves; you have been fretting
after a dear grandmother, who does not fret
for you. The dead are so ungrateful; it is
the only fault I have to find with them.
And now you want to get right away, out
of sight even of Droigel, with whom you
were angry last night—why, he does not
know, unless it is because he doubted

whether you had got your money's worth for your money. Never mind ; smile, smile again, Miss Annie, and I will declare you have had six copper pennies in exchange for every silver sixpence. We are friends once more, is it not so ?" and coming behind my chair, he laid a great hand on each of my shoulders, and stood in that attitude until I was forced into saying we were, and I hoped always should be, friends.

Hearing which, Herr Droigel sighed heavily.

"Your tone is not hearty, Miss Annie. You have got a fit of the English reserve. You are not transparent like me. You have some second thought. You are angry, and I know not why. Never mind," he added, cheerfully ; "some day I shall know—some day, when miss understand how truly and entirely I am her friend."

What answer could I make to this ? What could I say, save in a fit of remorse—

" I am not angry.   I am only foolish ; I am out of tune."

" Ah, how clever that is !" he soliloquized in an audible whisper.   " Out of the depths of her feminine temper she speaks to me as a musician.   How good it is !—a string loose, a string broken ; no matter who sweep the keys, a discord results.   Yes, she is right.   She wants to be in tune, and then all would be sweet as once it was."

Yielding to the influence of this judicious flattery, I permitted myself to be led back into the paths of good humour.   Once, indeed, I actually laughed, and I could not help noticing my uncle's look of pleased surprise at the sound.

" Will you dine with us to-day ?" he asked.

" No," answered Herr Droigel.   " I have principle, I have feeling.   If the good doctor asks me to stay with him year after year, as he does, I say to myself, ' Droigel, you are part of this dear man's family.   You go

not out to eat, you go not out to drink while
there.   You make not a lodgment of his
house.'   But if you or any other like to
request the pleasure of my society altogether for two—three days, good ; I say
not then no.'

"Will you give us the pleasure of your
society " (alas, I fear he found me dull !)
" for two or three days ?" asked my uncle,
eagerly.

"Let us talk about that as we walk,"
answered Herr Droigel, gravely; and the
pair took their hats and sallied forth.

I went with them as far as the gate, and
watched for a minute as they sauntered
across the green.   Suddenly Herr Droigel
turned and came hurrying back to where I
stood.

"You will make a great try, Miss Annie,"
he said, "to be like your own bright self of
a year ago.   It is so much trouble, I know,
for both ; but think, think how bad it is for
him."

And without giving me time to answer, he was gone, leaving me with ample food for thought during his absence.

The longer I thought, the more unendurable became the idea of changing the life I was leading for an existence cabined and confined by the rules and regulations of Mrs. Mitchell's establishment for young ladies. I was loyal to my grandmother's prejudices. Honestly I meant to adhere to my resolution of singing no more for ever ; and yet still I believe, had Herr Droigel asked me that evening to uplift my voice, I should not, to quote his own words, have said no.

Herr Droigel, however, was a great deal too astute to ask anything of the kind. Taking my statement apparently as final, he never mentioned my voice, he never spoke to me about music ; but he came and stayed at the cottage for two days, and during that time he played and sang, with many apologies, as he said, " to please himself, to pass the time."

" I shall interfere not with you, Miss Annie," he would remark. " While you are making your puddings, giving out your stores, marking your linen, I will amuse myself arranging one so simple melody. I will play soft, so as not to disturb a little baby ; and when you have thrown off your household cares and return, I will shut the instrument : not a note shall jar upon you."

What a stupid little fool I was ! I used to listen outside the door while he played, taking in fresh life, fresh thoughts, fresh health, and yet I would not turn the handle and, going up to him, say, " Herr Droigel, music is the breath of my breath. I cannot live without it. I put my future in your hands. Tell me what I must make of it."

The old influence was upon me, only stronger than of yore ; yet I could not, now the restraining hand was withdrawn, "gang mine ain gait" with the smallest pleasure; and knowing all this, luxuriating in the struggle he comprehended was going on, Herr Droigel only said calmly—

"What a pity miss does not care for music as she once did! It would be useful for her, if she is to teach all manner of accomplishments to English heiresses."

"Uncle," I said at length one evening, when a remark to this effect seemed to have drawn blood from every vein in my heart, "you hear what Herr Droigel says; you know what I feel; you understand what holds me back. If you were in my place, what should you do?"

There must have been some of the concentrated passion I felt evidenced in my manner, for my uncle looked up at me in surprise, whilst Herr Droigel maintained a discreet silence.

"What should I do, Nannie?" repeated my uncle. "You know my opinion of old. It has undergone no change."

"But oh, uncle, you told me always to be good to grannie."

"And were you not, my poor child?" he said. "If we all faithfully performed our duties as you did yours, there would be few aching hearts in the world, I fancy."

"But she did not want me to sing," I sobbed out.

"She could not sing herself, Nannie, and was unable to understand what the gift meant to you. She was a good woman, the best I ever knew," he added, speaking with a tremor in his voice which compelled his breaking off suddenly; "but," he went on, after a pause, "although she was so good and so true, we must not let our love blind us to the fact that her world was a small one, and that save through her love for you she never looked beyond it. I fancy, Nan," he said, by way of conclusion, "you, the stray lamb in our family, enlarged both our ideas. I never should have learnt toleration but for you."

"Hear!" exclaimed Herr Droigel, in a fat tenor.

"But, uncle," I said, unheeding that mark of approval, "if you were in my place, what should you do?"

"I should state my wishes to my friends, dear, and be guided by their advice. As for the dead"—once again he paused, but proceeded almost immediately—"I should consider the spirit of her wishes, instead of examining the letter. What my mother desired you to be, Nannie, was a good and happy woman. To my thinking you will be both good and happy if you use to the uttermost the gift God has given you. Had you become a great singer in her lifetime, no one would have felt more pride in the fact than my mother. She would have sat in the reserved seats, and whispered to her neighbour with modest pride, 'That is my granddaughter.'"

"Bravo!" exclaimed Herr Droigel.

"Then do you mean to say you think I

ought to take to music as a profession?"
I asked, breathlessly.

"I think you have a gift," he answered.
"I know you are in such a position that, if
you have a gift and can make money out of
it, you are bound to do so."

"And if *she* can look down?" I asked,
after a pause.

"If she can, it will be with eyes from
which the film of human prejudice has been
removed. She can either see our affairs
clearly now, Nan, or not at all."

"Then what ought I to do, uncle?"

"Ask Herr Droigel?"

"Herr Droigel, what ought I to do?"

"If Droigel were anything but a drivel-
ling fool, he would say, 'Miss Annie, what
are your affairs to me? Do what pleases
you best.' Oh, you women, young and old,
you are all alike. You take a man, and
fling him away, soh! in your pretty tempers. When you want his help—and that
is often—you go and pick him up and wind

him round your finger, and ask his advice. Fortunate it is for your sex that we are simpletons ; that we are without understanding, as the Bible says ; that you can put bits in our mouths, and drive us here, there, everywhere. What ought you to do ? you ask, Miss Annie. What you like, I reply ; and that is what you will do ; and you will get some foolish man, like Mr. Motfield and me, to help you at every step. To-morrow you shall come to me and say what you want, or rather I shall come to you and hear what you want. To-night I want, with your most gracious permission, to try the effect of a song I wrote to-day under the mulberry-tree of that dear Packman. May I, without offence, open your instrument ? Ten million thanks and apologies. Now I will sing."

He sang ; and, closing my eyes, I listened. It may seem ridiculous, but I never could bear to look at Herr Droigel when he was singing. The voice was the voice of an archangel; the body whence it proceeded was as unwieldy as that of an elephant—a mountain of soft, flabby, unpleasant fat flesh.

If memory serve me rightly, it is in one of Miss Edgeworth's tales that an account is given of a young lady who—disgusted with the prosaic comfort of her own home, and charmed with the ethereal view of life taken by a certain sentimental authoress in whose works she delighted, over whose touching sentences she wept—entered into a correspondence with the gifted one, and finally left her home; and, to the surprise and dismay of the gifted one, appeared in due course of time at the G. O.'s abode, which turned out to be rooms over a pastry-cook's shop.

To have dreamt of roses and honey-suckles, to have visioned an ideal home, where the jasmine shone faintly, and the nightingale sang in the myrtle-groves to his mate, and to awake to a fearful reality of bath-buns and raspberry-tarts, was sufficiently trying. Nevertheless there have been those who, in their adversity, lent a charm even to currant-loaves and preserves.

Of such, however, was not the author of those touching tales. She appeared frouzy as concerned her hair, untidy as to her dress, and—may it be spoken?—given to dram-drinking.

The young lady, repentant, returned to her friends, and was disillusioned and restored to the paths of practical, if monotonous, morality, after Miss Edgeworth's favourite fashion.

I often think of that delightfully priggish authoress when I recall Herr Droigel's music. By all her rules of prudence and morality—seeing him eat, seeing him drink, beholding that too large body moved to deeds of agility and locomotion—I ought to have forsworn music at once and for ever. I should have said, " Of what value is music,

if it can be content with such a habitation ?"
But I did no such thing.

Perhaps, indeed I know, I lamented the
setting in which that divine voice was presented ; but the voice seemed divine, for all
that.   Nevertheless I preferred shutting
my eyes to the source whence it proceeded.

I was then unaware that when the gift is
given, it is rarely provided with a casket to
match.   I had not then learned that porter,
or even white soup, was a good thing for
the voice.   Like a simpleton, I would here
below have separated the soul from the
flesh, had such a divorce been possible, and
listened to the spirit sounds without the
intervention of an unromantic body.

How that man sang !   I do not believe
he loved music one-half so well as I, and yet
his life was a long melody.

"That will do," he said, when the last
note died away, and he took his soft
fingers off the keys ; "that will bring
down the galleries.   I never care," he went

on, speaking to my uncle, "in this your practical England, for the applause of white gloves. I love to hear the stamp of strong boots, and see madame, in a discreet bonnet, nodding approval in her unbecoming way. Then I know I shall be whistled in the streets, sung by the middle-class million. When I write for the future —for fame—I send to mine own beloved country, and get, not money, but applause."

"Why do you not always write for applause?" I inquired.

"Because, my sweet Miss Annie, spite of that cynical Frenchman's remark, 'I see not why' in answer, one must live. Sometimes —yes, indeed, occasionally for a very long time—butcher and baker and candlestick-maker, as your distich has it, are forbearing and forgetful to an extent ; but another time comes, when one says, 'I want money to go to market,' and another, 'My miller must be paid,' and a third, 'The Herr from whom I buy tin and brass asks for a

few pounds.' So there comes the inevitable
hour of payment. Ah, if one could live on
fame!—if one could! But, alas, although
the money itself seems base—base—the
goods money can buy are not to be despised.
Now," proceeded this plausible individual,
"suppose that, instead of only having a
voice fit to sing in this small room, or in
one twice its size, I had an organ like that
nature has given to ungrateful Miss Annie,
and I could, so to speak, breathe golden
guineas, do you think I would indite songs
for young ladies to sing? *Ach nein!* But
it is always thus. Where the gift is not, it
is longed for; where it exists, it is spurned."

And then he executed an impromptu
mazurka, full of unexpected surprises, and
quaint strange changes of key; breaking
out, after that, into one of the songs of the
beloved Fatherland, which must have
sounded weird and strange to any English
person crossing our village green in the
calm twilight.

For me, all through that summer's night, I lay awake talking to the dead ; rehearsing my position to ears deaf, I trust, to earthly sounds. As I never could have spoken to her while living, I spoke to her then ; confident that if she understood anything, she understood all ; and when, towards morning, slumber stole away my waking senses, I dreamed that we were back in the old home at Lovedale, and that, with hand laid on my head, she was telling me to be a singer, if I liked.

"Only be good, Annie—only be good," she said in conclusion ; and with those words ringing in my ears I awoke.

Other sounds than dream voices, I soon found, had contributed to arouse me. Uncle Isaac was knocking vehemently at my door, and exclaiming—

"Nannie, do you *never* intend to get up ? Herr Droigel has been down for an hour past. He has eaten a dozen nectarines and a quart of mulberries, and now says he is ravenous for breakfast."

"Do not wait for me," I called out. "Give him a gallon of milk and a quartern loaf. I shall be dressed directly."

My heart felt lighter than it had done for weeks past, and I spoke out of its gladness. I felt so thankful at the prospect of being delivered from Mrs. Mitchell and her establishment; and yet still dreading I might be unmindful of grannie, seemingly forgetful of her, I was forced to murmur—

"Oh, grannie, don't think me wicked! You know all about it now."

Sing in that house I imagined I never could, but I meant to sing out of it. I was like a bird longing for the wild woods. Never before—never had I seen a chance of fully gratifying my wishes, of walking along the road I longed to travel. Much trouble had I caused hitherto; trouble I meant to cause no longer. I had a gift, and I would use it. I would be a witch, and breathe golden guineas, to quote our German friend. I would do something to make my relations proud of me. If I were possessed of a four-leaved shamrock, why should I not weave my spells? Why should I not leave the cottage, and go out into the wide, wide world to seek my fortune, as other girls had done?

Why not, indeed? There had been but one obstacle; and time, and my uncle, and my own understanding were fast obliterating that.

Rapidly I dressed and arranged my hair, and gave one last glance at the glass to see I was presentable, before descending into the room, where Herr Droigel—fat, rosy, and innocent-looking—was sitting at the breakfast-table, complacently surveying the ruin he had wrought.

A child might have played with that contented giant then, and I took advantage of my opportunity.

"Herr Droigel," I began, "I have thought over all you said last night, and if you and my uncle still believe I ought to be a singer, I should like to be one."

"Spoke I not so?" asked the German, addressing his host. "Said I not this, 'Miss Annie wants to sing; she will come down all bright and pleasant, with her little tempers gone, and smiling, give us to comprehend she is willing now to do that which you choose—in other words, that which she wish to do herself?' Oh, what a delightful sex is woman! How steadfast, how unchangeable, and how charming even in her fickleness!"

Having concluded which sentence, Herr Droigel rose; and taking my face between his immense hands, kissed me first on one cheek and then on the other.

Had Herr Droigel's character been as well known a book to me then as it is now, I could have told him that it is an easy matter for a man to be steadfast and unchangeable if he love no other created being, if he acknowledge no Creator, save himself—if he be his own all in all—the alpha and the omega of his fears and his hopes. But in those days I was young, as the reader is aware, and I had not yet eaten of the fruit which teaches us that even fatness and apparent foolishness, joined to a thorough knowledge of music, are not convincing proofs that under the seeming innocence of a dove may not be hidden the subtle cunning of a serpent.

Herr Droigel was no serpent, however; he was merely a self-seeking money-worshipper; and believing I should be worth gold to him, he kissed me, as stated, to my surprise, and to Uncle Isaac's intense amusement.

Truth to tell, I think it was a relief to Uncle Isaac that at length my mind was made up. Since his mother's death, I had been to him something very much in the nature of a white elephant—a useful, not to say ornamental, animal, in some stations of life, but a decided encumbrance to a druggist and chemist in a seaport town, who could not take me back to his own home, and who could ill afford the time and expense involved in travelling backward and forward to mine.

So we were all pleased that morning : my uncle, because he could now consign me to the care of some one who, as he phrased it, knew more about girls and music than he ; Herr Droigel, for the simple reason (expressed) that he " hoped to see Miss Annie smile once more ;" and I, because I had compassed the wishes of both, and my own too.

Already in my heart, as in the churchyard, the grass had commenced to spring over my grandmother's grave. Well, it is no sign of want of love that time should wear away the sharp edge of grief, and clothe with flowers and verdure the naked earth. Not even now, though the wound is closed, the sorrow overpast, is the memory of that first, best, truest friend less dear to me than it was in the days when under the yew-tree I sat weeping and wailing for the dead, who could never, I knew, "return to me," but to whom I had forgotten " I might go."

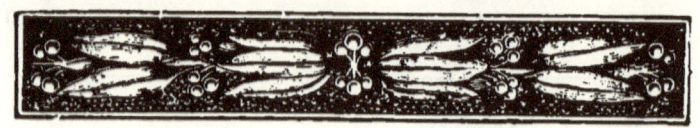

CHAPTER VII.

A NEW LIFE.

WHAT the pecuniary terms may have been upon which Herr Droigel undertook "to adopt me as Gretchen's sister and his own loved child and pupil," I cannot now remember.

Like everything else in which my uncle had a part, they were communicated to me at the time.

Impossible though the middle-aged may find it to realize, there is a time of life when money seems the least good in existence—when pounds, shillings, and pence form no part of youth's dreams, whether sleeping or waking—and it did not matter to me how much of my little fortune was to be spent in following that vision which had been silently beckoning me for years.

All I am now able to recollect about the matter is, that my uncle considered the remuneration Herr Droigel required extremely reasonable. And reasonable, so far as represented by figures, I do not in the least doubt it was. The German was to board and lodge me, to instruct me in music, and to "love me as his own"—he added this last item verbally—for some small amount which seemed to my uncle absurdly low; but then, as my new proprietor remarked with airy generosity—

"If Miss has the sad fate of losing her voice—of disappointing the rich and pigheaded British patron—of disliking the artiste life, which is at once so social and so lonely, so grand in itself, so low in the misconstructions of the ignorant—I do not wish that she shall return to this peaceful village—a beggar rendered penniless by Droigel. No, I name a price which means no loss to her, no gain to me. I put Miss Annie on the road to fortune. If she likes the road and is able to walk it, Droigel will share her success. If not, why then Droigel will have no reason to fear the dead grandmother waking him at night, by asking what he has done with the little one's portion.

"I speculate, in fact," he proceeded, after an instant's pause, devoted doubtless to a contemplation of the ghostly presence he had himself conjured up. "I have come on 'Change. Here is a possible, a probable voice. See, I will teach it, I will feed it, I will house it, I will nurse it, I will give myself much trouble; and then, if it make money, I shall go gleaning in its harvest time; if it make not money—then it cannot be helped; it will be a pity, that is all."

Whereupon Dr. Packman clapped his friend's immense shoulder, and said, "You are a fine fellow, Droigel;" and my uncle holding out his hand, remarked he considered it a privilege to have known him; in answer to which demonstrations of admiration Herr Droigel turned towards the window, wiped his eyes with a silk pocket-handkerchief, and then took a pinch of snuff out of Dr. Packman's box, and blew his nose loudly.

For me, I was in a seventh heaven of delight. Once the matter was settled, Herr Droigel left me no time for regret.

"The sooner Miss Annie begins her London career the better," he explained. "I do not mean to set her hard at work immediately. She will want to see the sights. We will go down to the river, where the mighty ships lie at anchor; she must visit the Tower; we will show her the Queen's palace, and all those great parks and wide streets, empty now, but filled in the season with lords and ladies, fine carriages, shining horses, footmen brilliant as paroquets. She shall behold

London with nobody in it,—bah! nobody except some two million souls; she shall meet more people in ten minutes than in this quiet Eden in ten months, and still she will see nobody, not till the season recommences, not till the Opera opens, not till I take her into fairyland, where rank and beauty congregate to listen to those so divine strains."

Uncle Isaac was glad also at the idea of my leaving Alford. He wanted to be back in his shop, to return to his buying and selling, to making fortunes and earning livelihoods for those children of whom his quiver was so full.

Already he had given me much of his time, and he was thankful, I believe, to feel that at length his responsibility was shifted to other shoulders.

Nevertheless, when the hour of parting came he took me in his arms and held me close, as if afraid to let me go. Afterwards he told me that for a moment he felt as if he must recall his permission, as if it were too great a risk to let me thus go forth amongst strangers, a poor slight bark upon the waters of an unknown sea.

But then he remembered it would all have'to be gone over again at some future period; that I had no home I could stay in, no friends I could live with; that a change had been wrought by death which pre-vented a return to the former course of things; and so he restrained himself, and said, "Nan, you are going out into a new life, but do not forget the old; you will make new friends, but never mistrust those you are leaving behind you. If you are unhappy, if you dislike your life in any way, write to me frankly, freely, fully. No one shall see your letters except myself." And then he kissed me over and over again, and so we parted.

"Weep, little one; never mind Droigel," said the Professor, compassionately. "It is a great big world this; but there is always

some tiny piece of its earth that seems
fairer to us than any other part, be the
other ever so beautiful.   There are millions,
billions, trillions of human beings fretting
and fuming their little day; but there is
always one human being of whom the heart
is fonder than of any other of the millions.
I understand all that.   I am fat and old;
but I have had my tears, and my soul-
aches—ach, yes !"

This permission and encouragement were
kindly meant, but had at once the effect of
stopping all outward evidence of my grief.
It is human nature, I suppose, to do that
which it is told not to do—not to do that
which it is told to do; and it was my
human nature not to care to indulge in a
grief such as had ever been gone through
by Herr Droigel.   I was still young enough
to believe my own griefs to be entirely my
own property; and if, by exhibiting them,
part possession came to be claimed by other
people, I decided it was better to conceal

those treasures with which I desired no one to intermeddle.

Unconsciously was beginning that dislike and distrust of sentimentality, of feelings worn on the sleeve, which stood me in such good stead in after life. I felt grateful towards Herr Droigel for his good intentions; but I was too old to like the notion of that huge German wiping (figuratively) my tears away.

If a girl or a woman be not hysterical, she can cease crying if she choose. I was not hysterical, and at the end of Herr Droigel's sympathetic speech my eyes were dry. Whereupon he recommenced his individual generalizing. I know no other combination of English words that will express my meaning.

"How beautiful is the adaptability of youth!" he said, addressing everybody generally, and me, for want of a better listener, in particular. "What a provision of a bountiful Heaven, that the heavier the

10—2

shower the sooner it is over! Consider
this, Annie : how long is it since I found you
weeping, like Rachel, not indeed for your
children, but for your dear grandmother,
who was more to you than many children?
You refused to be comforted ; you had but
one pleasure, to sit on the grass and cry.
Life had stopped himself for you. But
time went on nevertheless, and the Miss
Annie I knew first singing her little songs,
is now walking hand in hand with Droigel,
to begin a new life—a life so beautiful!"

Herr Droigel described literally our way
of proceeding. Hand clasped in hand, like a
couple of children, or a pair of simpletons, we
were crossing the field-paths to Great Alford.

He had made it a point, that when I left
the cottage I should leave likewise old
associations and old faces.

"I do not want to have the leave-
takings," he said. "When she bids 'good-
bye' to the place, let her bid 'good-bye' to
the loved friends too; after that trust

all to Droigel." The result of which was, that our luggage having been sent over to Great Alford, we followed after in the absurd fashion I have mentioned.

There was no one there to see, however, and holding my small hand in his great one seemed to please the Professor; so " hand in hand " we walked on together, whilst Herr Droigel poured forth quarts of conversational froth.

My experience of Germans was limited at that period—so limited, indeed, that Herr Droigel happened to be the only one with whom I had hitherto held converse; nevertheless my first experience warrants my last theory—namely, that let the circumstances under which one is placed with a German be what they will, he is certain to talk.

The determination of the natives of that country to say something, when no human being wants them to say anything, is perfectly marvellous. As a rule they reserve all their thoughts for books or business; as a rule they are totally destitute of any sense of humour ; but certainly as a rule they talk, or, perhaps, it would be better to say, babble. The stream is level and uninteresting ; it is not fetid, it is not wise ; it is certainly not witty, though a perfectly unembarrassed mind may contrive to be amused with, not at it.

The mystery would be why so astute a people should so seek to clothe themselves with a cloak of want of tact and dulness, were it not that the world may safely believe the Germans know their own business best.

Herr Droigel did, at all events, and babbled on sweetly concerning the infinite wisdom and mercy of a Providence in whose existence I have not the slightest reason to suppose he believed, until we reached the coach which was to convey us the first part of our way to London.

Railways have not yet arrived at the length of delivering passengers at every house ; then there were several towns they did not condescend to notice. Great Alford was one of those neglected. From that place to the nearest station we travelled by coach.

On that coach—for we travelled outside, and I liked the journey—Herr Droigel made himself agreeable to guard and driver, and to his fellow-passengers. He spoke of me as his daughter, and people were kind in consequence. When we left the conveyance, it struck me, however, that both guard and coachman were not quite satisfied at sight of the extremely small coin of the realm with which he rewarded their services. Perhaps I was mistaken; perhaps his manner, lordly and free, had unduly raised their expectations.

At the station this impression was not reproduced : porters are thankful for extremely small gifts, and the twopence Herr Droigel gave—I know it was twopence, for I saw the amount placed in the hand of a servant of the company—seemed to afford that servant satisfaction,—perhaps because it was in contravention of the company's rules.

Anyhow he took the twopence, and we were all pleased—I especially; because the surly looks of guard and driver had somewhat discomposed my equanimity.

For the second time in my life I was in a railway carriage. How green the fields looked—how strange the hedges hurrying by—how frightened the cattle scurrying off at our approach—how wonderful the thronged stations—how strange it seemed to lose passengers and to gain others. What a new world to me.

But after a few hours I grew tired of it. Nobody knew me, nobody cared for me, nobody looked at me, nobody spoke to me, save occasionally Herr Droigel, who slept a good deal, and got out at all the stations and made ineffectual attempts to open up conversations with fellow travellers who obviously distrusted and feared foreigners, and responded in monosyllable; and so at last when evening closed in, I too fell asleep, and was only wakened by a horrible clamour, which

when I roused myself and listened atten-
tively, meant, I found—

"Tickets ready—all tickets here!" Then
after a few minutes' panting and racing and
screaming, the engine slackened speed and
some one one said—

"This is London;" and again I rubbed my
eyes, and alighted.

In one of Miss Edgeworth's innocent
plays, a boy is made to say—"I cannot see
the town for houses."

Miss Edgeworth in this sentence exactly
defined my feelings at first sight of London.

I could not understand it; and as we
drove through street after street, and then
through more streets, I who had never
realized what a great city means, felt like
the man who coming to a rapid river, sat
down on the bank waiting for the stream
to cease flowing. I was waiting to come to
some place "where I could see the town,"
when our conveyance stopped.

"Welcome to your new home, beloved

Annie !" and so speaking, Herr Droigel led me up three steps and into a narrow hall, where we were met by a woman and a girl, whom Herr Droigel greeted, to my intense astonishment—I had learnt enough of his language to understand the meaning of a few substantives—as his wife and daughter.

That Madam Droigel! *that* Gretchen! I could have wept, but that past experience had convinced me weeping was useless. Had I been possessed of sufficient courage, I should have rushed after our departing vehicle, and said, " Take me, oh, pray take me anywhere out of this world !"

There was a large woman, without collar or tucker, who was kissed by Herr Droigel—a woman made and clothed in defiance of all rules then accepted, poor as, by comparison with the present, was the best code of dress then known. There was Gretchen, untidy likewise—untidy beside me.

Very much the advantage I felt at that moment of my well-fitting dress—the young

and slight are so easy to fit : my neatly-
pleated crape trimmings—my sorrowful
bands—my close mourning bonnet, from
which, no doubt, a pale face looked out
sorrowfully.

"How do you do, dear afflicted Miss
Annie ?" said the woman without a tucker,
kissing me with lips that smelt of garlic,
and then presenting a full cheek in order
that I might return her greeting.

"How do you do, dear ?" said Miss
Gretchen, rubbing her face against mine.
"Aren't you tired ? Come upstairs. Should
you like to have supper first, and go to bed
afterwards ; or go to bed first, and have
supper afterwards ?"

"I should like, if I might do so, to go to
bed and have no supper," I answered, feebly.

"Just as you please, dear one."

"Thou art weary, is it not so ?" asked
Madam Droigel, laying her plump hands on
my shoulder. "Yes, go to bed, and I myself
will bring thee up a cup of tea."

"No, muder," interposed Gretchen, whose life was, as I found afterwards, spent in mimicking her father and mother's forms of speech. " I myself mean to wait upon Miss Annie. She is to have everything she wants, and nothing she does not want—to-night," added the young lady, with an ominous accent on the last word. "Is it not so ?" she asked, turning to her father.

" To-night and all days and nights Miss Annie shall have everything she wants that I can give her," said Herr Droigel, with paternal tenderness. " My child, you are worn out. Go with my Gretchen. Gretchen, be tender to this little fragile bud."

" The bud shall be tenderly handled by me," answered his daughter ; and so saying, she led the way up to a room on the second floor, where, in the midst of a desert of bare boards, there was placed a small bedstead, a painted chest of drawers (above which hung a little glass), a rush-bottomed chair, a washhand-stand—provided with a jug about the size of a cream ewer, and a basin no larger than a soap-cup—completed the furniture of this apartment.

"You will be happy here ?" It is due to Miss Gretchen's common sense to say she asked the question doubtfully.

I could not answer. If I had opened my lips to speak, I must have burst out crying ; and I did not want to cry. I looked round the bare room, and contrasted it with my little chamber at Lovedale, my larger and prettier apartment at Alford.

Well, I had chosen ! I had decided to give up everything for music. I had gone too far to turn back again. I could not have everything.

"I will try to be happy," I said, after a pause, filled up by the thoughts indicated. "I am sure you are very kind. It would be a shame if I did not try to be happy."

"You would not like me, I suppose, to call you 'Bud' ?" suggested Miss Gretchen ; " and so I will not do it, though I shall always think of you in connexion with papa's simile. It must seem very strange to you at first. I only hope it will not all seem very disagreeable to you at last. I am so thankful you are not a foreigner; I do hate foreigners. Your predecessor was a foreigner. Good heavens, how delighted I was when one day she tore up her music, and boxed papa's ears! He can stand a great deal; but he did not like having his ears boxed and his face slapped; so we got rid of Mademoiselle in double-quick time. There never was an allegro movement so cleverly performed in this house."

"What was the matter—could not she learn ?" I inquired.

"She would not learn," answered Miss Gretchen. "Papa said she might have done anything, if she had only been industrious; but she was lazy to her very bones —lazy, and greedy, and ill-tempered. She once boxed my ears, but she did not attempt it a second time. She wanted me to wait upon her, and I would not. She used to call us all devils, as calmly as if there were nothing unusual in such a mode of address. But I am keeping you up. I will leave you now, and come back in a quarter of an hour to see if you will drink that cup of tea I doubt not my mother is already brewing."

"Tell me," I said, detaining her, "tell me before you go, what you meant downstairs when you remarked I was to have all I wanted to-night. Is Herr Droigel very, very severe?"

"Papa is not cross, if that is what you mean," the girl replied. "He lets me do as I like. He would let you do as you like, if you did not, unluckily for yourself, happen to have a voice; but as you have a voice, you will find him—how shall I put it?—strict. You will have to serve your voice, if you can understand me; eat for it, drink for it, walk for it, sleep for it, work for it; and if you are not particularly fond of your voice, you may find all this slightly tiresome. For me, I am humbly thankful to the Almighty for not having given me the slightest ear for music."

"I heard your father once make the same remark," I observed; "but he implied that you were not so satisfied about the matter as he."

"My father is one of the most truthful men living," said Gretchen, calmly; "to quote his own expression, he is transparent; but still you must not take everything even he says literally. There, I knew how it would be," she continued, rushing to the door as a mellow cry of "Gretchen, mine own child!" came up the staircase. "That is to tell me the Bud must not be exhausted by conversation," she explained, and having so explained left me at last alone.

Herr Droigel was as good as his word. He did not put harness on, and begin to drive me immediately. He took me to see the sights. We went up the river and down it. We made so regular a business of pleasure, that I soon got tired, and was glad when lessons began in earnest.

But oh, what those lessons grew to be! what that study of music proved! what the cultivation of my voice really meant!

Most persons have an idea that nothing is so easy as to sing a song; unless, indeed, it may be to write a book. When they hear of some prima donna receiving so much a note, they shake their heads and say—

"People who work hard cannot earn money so easily as that."

Whilst the fact is, there are no people who have to work so hard as those who earn their bread by discoursing sweet sounds.

It is, indeed, utterly impossible for any person outside the musical profession to form the faintest idea of the drudgery which must be gone through before even a small success can be achieved. The un-initiated hear what the prima donna is paid per note, but they can never know what that note cost the prima donna.

No one either can ever know what my notes cost me; the toil, the vexation of spirit. I shudder when I recall those lessons. I sicken at the memory of Herr Droigel's despair when he found that, physically, I was unable to bear the burden of the tasks he put upon me. I seem to dread once more the sound of the word "health," and, ill with nothing but utter exhaustion, I lie again on my bed, with Gretchen bathing my temples with eau-de-cologne, and renewing her thanks to Providence that it was not of the least use her father ever attempting to teach her to sing.

And yet, in spite of all the work and all the hardship, I was happier than I had ever been in my life before. I drank-in music, and I was content. The vague longings, the yearning for something my lot did not hold, were satisfied at length.

Youth makes little account of want of

bodily comfort, so long as heart and soul are filled. My heart was not empty. I had long letters, tender and wise, from my uncle. I made friends, as he prophesied would be the case. I grew very fond of Gretchen, and she at length grew so fond of me, that out of pure love she brushed her hair, and kept her shoes up at heel, and mended her dresses, and would have made the house tidy, had father or mother wished it to be so.

But neither father nor mother had the slightest desire for anything of the kind.

They were never happy if by chance their surroundings were in order. They rejoiced to live in a perpetual hurricane of disorder. Herr Droigel did the cooking. When he was not eating, smoking, singing, or teaching, or sleeping, he was in the kitchen. Madame Droigel did nothing. During the entire time I lived in that house, I never saw her even attempt to do anything, unless, indeed,. to assist in laying the cloth.

The rooms were kept in order, or supposed to be kept in order, by a succession of small maids-of-all-work, who might, judging from their innate depravity, capacity for breakage, grimy countenances, and unkempt locks, have all been eggs out of one nest.

Jane went, and Sophy succeeded, and Kate followed after; but there was no difference, except in name. They were all, as Madame Droigel, who set them such an admirable example, remarked, "idle sluts" —in vituperation, Madame's English was remarkably strong.

Once we had a grown-up servant—trim, active, cleanly ; a being so superior to all who had gone before, that, hearing Gretchen's report, I went down into the basement to have a look at her.

There she was, actually scrubbing out the pots. For thirty-six hours we retained that treasure. At the end of that period she had threatened to pin the dishcloth to Herr Droigel's coat-tails. She had requested Madame Droigel to place her on board-wages, in order that she might procure some food fit for a Christian (meaning herself) to eat. She had informed Gretchen that where she lived previously, when young ladies wanted anything they rang for it, and did not scream after servants as she did ; whilst she took the duster, wherewith it had been my wont to employ my few leisure minutes in the mornings, into her possession, intimating at the same time her opinion that I had enough work of my own to do, without interfering with hers.

As for Gretchen and myself, we would thankfully have complied with her wishes, and told her so, with a deference which, I think, touched her feelings. But Herr Droigel could not consent to leave her in undisputed possession of the kitchen ; and Madame was hurt at her expressed opinions

on the subject of foreign messes. So she
departed, and we returned to our Janes
and Sophias and Kates.

Herr Droigel that evening prepared for
our delectation a dish more unspeakably
nasty than it had yet fallen to my lot to
taste; whilst Madame his wife donned—
probably in honour of being mistress in her
own house once more—a black-silk dress so
hopelessly denuded of hooks, that even she
was fain to hide its gaping back from sight
by means of a faded crape shawl.

CHAPTER VIII.

AN OLD FRIEND.

SO far from finding that the lapse of time reconciled me to the peculiar habits of Herr Droigel and his wife, intimate association with them only produced a feeling of greater and ever greater amazement.

For days and days together, Herr Droigel, so active a pedestrian at Alford, would not stir outside the hall-door; and when his "stay-at-home fit," as Gretchen called it, was on him, he never thought it necessary to wash or shave, or even dress.

I have been privileged to see that now distinguished Doctor of Music in the very scantiest raiment a human being could well

go about in—as near nudity, in fact, as our
absurd civilization would permit.

At first I was surprised and shocked, if
so strong an expression befits the circumstance ; but I soon began to consider that
if Herr Droigel did not mind his *déshabille,*
why should I ?

He was the person who ought to have
felt disconcerted ; and if, so far from being
disconcerted, he revelled in it, would it not
have been presumptuous for me to set up
my judgment in opposition to his ?

Once—it was late on an autumn afternoon—a brougham drove up to our door,
and a gentleman alighted, who was shown
into the drawing-room, and who gave a
name to the servant which was evidently
unfamiliar to my master.

With many groans, and Gotts, and
Himmels, the Professor betook himself to
his bedroom, whilst Gretchen rushed downstairs for warm water, and Madame hurried
upstairs, rending her dress on a nail by

the way, to look her beloved out clean linen.

He had shaved himself; he had got on a pair of black trousers; he was about to incase his feet in boots, when suddenly a cheery voice resounded through the house.

"Droigel! Droigel! why the deuce don't you come to me? I can't wait for you all day."

As when a soldier, preparing to meet an enemy, hears the familiar watchword, beholds an accustomed uniform, changes his defensive attitude, so the Professor, at sound of that voice, dropped his boots, resumed his slippers, and in all the glory of a clean shirt, destitute of a collar, and wristbands still unbuttoned, darted from his room.

Not for me is it to chronicle the expressions with which that usually peaceable man prefaced his sentence. Suffice it to say that neither Gott nor Himmel had any part or parcel in them.

"Why did you not say who you was, that so I need not to have dressed?" he asked, and there was an agony of reproach in his voice, which seemed, however, to fail in touching his hearer's sympathies.

"Dressed! by Jove, I don't know about that!" was his visitor's reply. "Seems to me you couldn't have much less on, unless you were in your birthday garments."

Then the door shut, and Gretchen, standing on the top of the first flight of stairs, and I, standing in the hall, burst into a peal of laughter, which I afterwards knew elucidated from Herr Droigel the remark—

"There goes my babies; they must have their laugh at the fat papa."

It always seemed to me a pity that Madame Droigel did not join together, or permit us to join together, two of her black quilted petticoats for her husband's use. Had she done so, I am sure he would have donned the garment with a charming unconsciousness of any ridicule which might appear to attach to it, and waddled about the kitchen in a state of intense delight. As it was, he prepared various delicacies for our table in a dress, or rather undress, the particulars of which would scarcely bear reproduction here, and which filled me, as I have said, with an ever-increasing sense of amazement.

Cannot I, glancing over my shoulder from the square pianoforte before which I was seated, see him now, ay, and hear him, as from the fireplace, where he is concocting some particularly nasty culinary mess, he bellows an entreaty for me to mind what I am about or a malediction on any specially pernicious vocal habit into which I have fallen.

Once again I behold the worn, greasy, shabby grey dressing-gown fastened round his ample waist by a cord formerly composed of strands of many colours, but now faded and dirty; the slippers, old friends, old and trusted, well tramped down at the heel, are a visible presence; over them hang socks, put on but never pulled up; and then, towering above all, the self-made drawbacks of his life, and his belongings, and his dress, rises the large grand head, which holds so much knowledge, worldly and otherwise, and has, to my thinking, made so little out of it all.

His intellect, his genius, his art, were sufficient to invest even that untidy house with a charm of novelty and romance.

His disquisitions on disinterestedness, upon the abominable characteristics of selfishness, upon the detestable nature of people who told untruths, delighted, and I regret to say, imposed upon me.

Viewing his character calmly, after the lapse of years—looking at him through the grey-tinted neutral glasses with which Time kindly provides most of us—I think Herr Droigel's three strong passions were love of eating, love of ease, love of money.

I do not believe any one predominated over the other. If he had a fourth passion, it was one so characteristic of all his compatriots, that it seems scarcely worth mentioning : he loved diplomacy.

So to speak, he never passed through a gate when there was a gap in a hedge he could creep through, or a roundabout path he could traverse ; but then this is characteristic of his nation. Perhaps it is one cause of their supremacy at the present moment. Heaven grant it may be a very proximate cause of their downfall hereafter —the downfall of the nation at large, as it has proved over and over again of individuals composing that nation !

As for Madame Droigel, she was extracted from a depth of insufficiency which no pure German could, so far as my knowledge of the race extends, hope to fathom or understand.

She was the daughter of German parents, born in England—parents hard-working, but destitute of brains. Madame Droigel lacked both brains and the capacity for hard-work; and the result was the woman in whose house I became domesticated.

From this pair was eliminated Gretchen —a young lady who, like her father, loved ease, and who, when I first knew the Droigels, was fast following in the footsteps of her mother.

Out of the house, indeed, her apparel was gorgeous. She arrayed herself in the height of the fashion, whatever that fashion might chance to be. She affected the showiest colours, and was, indeed, in all respects, a very dashing and conspicuous young person.

Indoors, however, she was down at heel, collarless, untidy, grimy, until, as has been stated, out of pure love for me, she began mending her ways and her stockings, put in the typical stitch in time, dressed herself completely even for breakfast, and improved her general appearance so greatly, that Herr

Droigel bègan to survey her critically, and to exclaim regretfully—

"Hadst thou but possessed a voice, Gretchen, thou mightst have played at football with the world."

"But I do not care for football," answered easy-tempered, unambitious Gretchen. "Here is Annie, she shall achieve fame, and earn money enough for us all."

"Ah, child, our loved Annie has a sweet voice, and can sing her little songs when she is in the mood adorably ; but with your presence, ach, Himmel, what might you not have done ?"

"Gone on the stage, I presume," interrupted Gretchen. "Gone on the stage and screamed before the footlights. That is not my idea of happiness at all. I want to find somebody who has ten thousand a year, and get him to marry me, that I may have what I wish, and do nothing for the remainder of my life."

And Miss Gretchen tossed up her head,

clothed with its German glory of golden plaits, having thus explicitly stated her desires, whilst Herr Droigel, after taking once more a critical inventory of her charms, and considering how irresistible they would have proved in conjunction with a good voice, uttered a dolorous " Ach !" and relapsed into silence.

Not by any direct sentence, not indeed by any sentence at all, did Herr Droigel gradually impress upon me the fact that my " presence" was not one calculated to curry favour with the British public. I was quick enough to understand that though the life of a singer of ballads had once been the extent of his hopes for me, still a brief period ensued when he fancied London and himself might have stimulated and gratified me to aspire to higher flights still.

And he had to abandon that expectation. I should never be more than a singer of songs—able to earn my five or ten guineas for an evening—and then " evenings are not always," sighed Herr Droigel.

" God is good," he explained to me once ; " but he does not give to us everything we want." And then I fully understood that my master believed my voice and myself were mismated—that, to put it differently, but more plainly, had Herr Droigel been intrusted with my creation, he would have put my voice into Gretchen's body, or *vice versâ.*

In any event he would have conjoined the two.

As for Gretchen, she was, and it pleases me to add, is one of the most amiable of created beings. Go to her when you will, see her under any circumstances, meet her in any place, she is still charming. She is one of those fortunate beings who, having accepted no responsibilities, never meets you with an anxiety, present or anticipated, clouding her brow.

Golden hair, blue eyes, transparent com-

plexion, good features, a large well-de-
veloped person, and a calm heifer-like
demeanour, have in her case done wonders.

If she failed to reach the desired ten
thousand a year, at least she has done remarkably well in the matrimonial market.

Only the other evening we sat together
in her dressing-room—her maid was dis-
missed—her long fair hair floated placidly
over her shoulders ; the dear papa we knew
was smoking downstairs, and helping the
esteemed husband to empty the remains of
a specially esteemed bottle of cognac.

Peace reigned—the children, under the
charge of a highly-paid and respectable
nurse, slept the sleep of infancy, and Gretchen, large and calm, surveyed with com-
placent eyes the fire another's exertions had
kindled and kept lighted for her.

" A charming home this is, mia cara," I
remarked.

" Yes," she answered ; " and but for you
I should never have called it mine. When

I think of that home and myself as you first knew it and me, I blush; but you have been the most loyal of human beings; otherwise——" and she paused in a sort of horrified silence.

She will never read this book; she never reads anything, neither does her husband; thus far and a great deal farther they are well mated, and therefore I think I may say, without fear of contradiction, I made Gretchen Droigel.

All unwittingly, I, who had myself risen from so poor an estate, taught her *les convenances* of society—taught her that people who wish to conquer the world must consider its prejudices; instilled into her a belief that unkempt hair and careless dress are not merely untidy but impolitic; that in this world very few people in any rank can afford to be eccentric or natural, if their naturalness separate them in the smallest degree from their fellows.

I have been loyal to Gretchen. Through

me she made her mark, and has retained it unmolested ever since. She is not the bright, piquant companion I can recollect. Her sense of humour is blunted. Her ideas of propriety are strong. Altogether I do not care much for Gretchen now, and am always glad when her visits terminate. Nevertheless, artistic though my nature may be (she tells me it is so), I am sufficiently English to remember old times, and remembering, I am always rejoiced to see the carriage appear which is to bear Juno and her offspring away from my door.

It seems to me I breathe more freely even in a worse atmosphere. It seems to me I ought never to have been admitted into decent society, seeing how impatient I feel when the feet and the inches of social propriety are laid in measurement against my daily life.

The course of the existence I have to record, however, is not that of Gretchen. It is mine own.

Mine own as it was then—clipped of its sentiment, shorn of its romance, by Herr Droigel.

If I walked, he or Gretchen must accompany me ; if his friends called, he expected I should retire from the room ; if I went to church, he exacted a promise from me that I should sing no praises to the God who had been a very present help to me in trouble—a sufficient refuge from my earliest youth. Acquaintances of my own I had none : he gave me no chance of making any. I practised in a back room. I exercised my voice to the dismay of right and left neighbours who were undiscriminating.

During the time I lived with Herr Droigel, man did not hear, nor woman either, any of my " little songs." I know now that the Professor dreaded lest some one should snatch me out of his hand and reap the harvest he designed to garner for himself ; but then I accepted in good faith his statement that he feared my getting into bad habits, that he did not wish me to exert my voice unduly.

"When it is strong, quite strong, and you are strong also, then let us take the public into our confidence; but till then we must be careful so much."

Nevertheless, spite of all his caution, the fact that one of Herr Droigel's "babies" was destined for the musical profession oozed out. Curious glances began to be cast upon me; inquiries were made concerning me, as thus—

"I say, Droigel, who is that girl you keep so much in the background? She is not your child, I know. A wonder, eh?"

"She is mine child by adoption," the Professor answered; "and she is a wonder of goodness and amiability. She is alone in the world except for me and my wife and Gretchen, and an uncle so kind, so true. Poor little Annie!"

Whereupon his visitor burst into a fit of laughter, and exclaimed, "Bravo, Droigel!

You are inimitable; but what is the use of trying to humbug me? You are teaching the girl to sing, I suppose, and expect to make a pot of money out of her."

This Gretchen told me—this and other speeches like unto it—adding on her own account—

"I am dying to know when the curtain is to draw up, and the performance begin. Never before did I take the smallest interest in one of papa's pupils; but I would give anything to see you stand up and sing before thousands of people. I should be as nervous as mamma when she hears a mouse in the room."

"Has Herr Droigel had many pupils?" I inquired.

"Lots," was the answer—"lots that he has improved and finished; but not many from the beginning, like you. Once he picked up a pearl—Mdlle. Baroilhe. She was a wonder, I believe. I was a tiny bit of a thing at the time, and can scarcely remember her. But she made all our fortunes. She lost her voice the third season she appeared, and had to leave the stage; but papa had got a quantity of money out of her voice before that. We lived in a very different house from this then. Do you know we were once quite rich? But papa speculated, and lost all he had. He is always making and losing. If you turn out a success, he wont be in the least better off at the end of five years."

"Gretchen, suppose I should not be a success, what would your father say then?"

"He would never forgive you," she answered; "and for that matter, neither, I think, should I; for my heart is set on your achieving a triumph. But you musn't be afraid. Papa knows what he is about; and he would never have taken you on the terms he did, had he not been certain you would do well both for yourself and him. Of course, as you are not being trained for the stage, you will never make a success like Mademoiselle; but papa's idea is, I fancy, to make you sing in oratorios and those sort of things. You will see if I am not right."

And so she went on chattering, quite unconscious that the desire of my heart was to sing on the stage, to utter those heart-thrilling notes I listened to with bated breath when uttered by others; for at last Herr Droigel had fulfilled his promise, and taken me to the Opera.

Never shall I forget that night. Three years I had been in London, and for some reason, which is still a mystery to me, my master, whilst always expressing his intention of giving his "little ones" a treat, seemed to make a point of deferring that treat as long as possible. One day, however, he begged "dear mamma" to make herself and us as handsome as possible.

"We go to hear Serlini," he explained; "and mine old pupil and still good friend Givorna has sent me a box. Ha, Miss Annie, what say you now!—long-wished for come at last. Such a treat! such an actor! such an actress! and, ach Gott, such singers too! We must all put on our best bibs and tuckers. Ah, you laugh! You are always laughing at Droigel. You are a naughty girl, Miss Annie, for all your grave face and demure little ways—always making fun of the fat old master who is teaching you so much."

"Don't get pathetic, papa," said Gretchen, "or you will make Annie cry." And then she took him round the neck, and kissed first one cheek and then the other, after which she executed a *pas seul* round the table, finishing her performances by waltzing me out of the room, in order to look up our finery.

"Ah, Heaven, what a pity! what a pity!" said the Professor, following her movements with a melancholy pride.

"That I have no voice," panted Gretchen, pausing. "It is a pity; for had I possessed one, I might have become another Serlini."

" Ach, no," answered her father ; " there is but one Serlini ; there will never be no other."

" The mould was broken up after she was created," remarked Miss Gretchen, gaily. " There is but one Serlini, and Herr Droigel is her prophet and Annie her worshipper."

" Will one of you two girls sew my body into my blue-silk skirt ?" asked Madame, in her broken English. Born in the country, she had never learnt to speak its language any better than her father and mother had done before her.

" Yes," answered Gretchen ; " one of us two girls—Annie, to wit—will perform the surgical operation you have mentioned."

Not without difficulty did we succeed in so dressing Madame as to render her presentable ; but when at length her toilette was completed, and Herr Droigel admitted to a private view, his satisfaction could

only find expression in a Babel of language
I dare not attempt to reproduce.

She was charming; she was beautiful as
in her first youth. No one would believe
she could ever have chosen such a fat
awkward husband as poor Droigel.

Proud girls were we as we looked and
listened and laughed. Happy girls when,
dressed in all our best, we squeezed ourselves together as Herr Droigel's huge
body, coming into the cab, tightened us up
as though he were a cramp.

"I don't believe it is real—I don't believe we shall ever get there," said Gretchen,
looking radiantly pretty.

She but expressed my feelings. I kept
tight hold of her hand, and had to say
perpetually to myself, "I am going to the
Opera," in order to feel I was not dreaming. I had done the same thing in Fairport years and years before. Had time
gone back? Was I walking once again
within sound of the murmuring sea? For

a moment as I closed my eyes the illusion seemed perfect, but when I opened them, wet with tears, I beheld the thronged streets, the bright gaslight, the thousands hurrying this way and that.

The night which came back to my memory so vividly had wrought all this change in my life. From quiet Lovedale to London was a transition not more extraordinary than that I, the country-bred child, reared in such seclusion, fenced round with prejudices and loving strictness, should be now in training for a public singer !

Let speculators build as many new operahouses as they please, they will never raise another edifice so dear to the hearts of a former generation as Her Majesty's.

It is all very well for young and flippant writers to speak of the Dust-hole in the Haymarket, but can they crowd another house with the memories and the traditions it contained ?

What actors and actresses have trod

those boards! what floods of melody have been poured forth under its roof! what stories, sinful and tragic and pitiful, have been played out behind the scenes! what gay, and witty, and sorrowful, and gloomy, and distinguished, and wicked men and women have jostled each other in the crush-room!

It was fitting that when the time came for the old house to pass away, fire should have been the agent for its destruction.

Who that loved Her Majesty's—and what veteran opera-goer failed to do so?—could have endured to behold the building torn limb from limb by callous workmen, its properties sold, its stage pulled down, its scenery carted off, its boxes sold for firewood?

" Better so," I believe, must have been the second thought of every man and woman who had memories connected with the dear old opera-house. The first thought natu-rally was one of regret; the next, that as its days could not in any event have been long in the land, it had perished so gloriously.

Fairyland had the poor little theatre at Fairport seemed to me that evening when I entered it with my uncle.

If there be a seventh heaven of fairyland, I entered it that night with Herr Droigel. To others the gilding and the paint might have seemed dingy and the curtains faded, but to me they were fresh, and bright, and beautiful.

We were all kings and queens and princesses in our box. Herr Droigel arrayed so carefully that it seemed impossible to associate him and the word *déshabille* together; Madame clad in many colours, a style of costume which suited her; Gretchen and myself simply attired as became our youth, but still dressed for the evening, and looking as well as our neighbours.

The opera was *Les Huguenots*. Shall I ever forget it as then performed, ever lose the memory of how Serlini sung, and Givorna sustained his part? To the end of my life I shall recollect the clapping, the encores, the bouquets, the frantic applause which greeted the prima donna.

"Ah!" exclaimed Herr Droigel, as she at length retired from the stage half concealed by flowers, "that is a life worth living for, the only life worth having."

As for me, I could not speak; my very soul seemed to have left me and gone out to seek that woman who, marvellous when I first heard her, had since developed powers which rendered Herr Droigel's remark of there being but one Serlini no exaggeration.

There never was her equal before, there never will be her equal again. Voice, culture, passion, pathos, beauty, grace, all these she combined in her own person.

She has gone, and left no copy of herself. Never for ever will another Serlini cross an English or any other stage.

After that night it so happened that other tickets were sent, and we went twice again that season to the Opera. Then Herr Droigel remarking that late hours and a summer in London were destroying his sweet Annie's good looks, we suddenly packed up and transported ourselves to the sea-side.

There, however, my lessons still continued. We had a detached cottage and a hired piano, and my master divided his time between composing music and finding fault with me.

"Depend upon it," said Gretchen, who understood the signs of her father's barometer, "he intends to bring you out next season. He is not quite satisfied as to the prudence of his determination, but he has resolved to risk the plunge."

"But if I should fail," I suggested.

"Psha!" she replied; "you wont fail unless you wish to do so. We all know that."

"But it is so soon," I murmured.

"It is like having a tooth out," she replied; "the sooner the operation is over the sooner you will be at ease. Listen to me, Annie," she went on. "You are one of those absurd girls who ought to have a father and mother and half a dozen brothers and sisters to maintain, in which case you would be so anxious to earn money that you would forget yourself and everything except money. Now you profess to be fond of me, and I believe you are; therefore, the moment you get up to sing, think, 'I am singing for Gretchen. If I succeed she will be happy; if I fail, times will not be good with her.' Say to yourself, 'I am singing to give Gretchen a *dot;* if I get an encore, that means happiness and ease to the Droigels. They have invested in me—if I turn out a poor affair, they lose both hope and money; whereas if I succeed we—they and I—will be rich and prosperous and content.'"

When I think over all this now, it seems to me that a portion at least of Herr Droigel's mantle had fallen upon Gretchen, that, like her father, she was wise in her generation; and yet, why should I blame the girl? She was getting, I doubt not, weary of comparative poverty, and she looked to me as a certain deliverer.

Still, if I failed! That idea was ever present with me whilst practising and taking my lessons; but whenever I could sing out the songs I fancied, all alone by myself, no doubt of success entered my mind.

Chafed and worn and mortified, and scolded by Herr Droigel, music was one thing. Sung as I listed—without teacher or critic—it proved quite another.

And in this way I was, one afternoon, screaming out to myself an *aria* from the last opera we had heard—shrieking, declaiming, in my own poor manner travestying the brilliant prima donna.

The house, to all intents and purposes, I

had to myself—for there was only one woman in it, and she nearly deaf.

Two days previously, Herr Droigel had, with many protestations of regret, and assurances of his unalterable attachment for us individually and collectively, left our temporary home for London.

Madame and Gretchen were out boating, and I was doing what I dared not have done had the Professor been within sound of my voice, trying over song after song, humming the easiest parts, skipping the most difficult, slurring over brilliant passages—" ganging my ain gait," in fact, in defiance of all commands, entreaties, and injunctions; and it is needless to add, enjoying myself thoroughly.

At length I came to one of the most lovely of operatic melodies—one which I had heard sung by Madame Serlini a short time before we left town.

As I played the symphony, every tone of voice, every turn of expression, seemed to come back to my memory; and flinging aside the repression I always felt when singing to Herr Droigel, I broke out with a power of voice and a strength of passion to which I had never before given utterance since I left Alford.

When the last note died away, as it was intended to do, in almost a sob, Herr Droigel put his head through the open window, and said—

"Go on."

Instead of going on, I jumped up from the piano, upset the music in my fright, and was essaying to collect the scattered sheets when my master entered the room.

"Go on," he repeated; "if you can sing like that, always sing the same—do you hear—repeat that for me similar once again."

He might as well have told me to stand on my head.

"What is the matter with you, child?" he exclaimed. "What are you trembling

about ? Why for do you fear Droigel ?
Am I a monster that you shake and shiver ?
Have I beat you ? have I spoken hard
words to you ? have I not been kind to you
as to Gretchen ? Come, tell me what it is
I have done that you can sing well the
moment my back is turned, and then, when
I do show myself, you turn white, as if you
did see one ghost."

"When I am singing to you," I answered, "I feel I am always going wrong."

"And so you do go wrong often, and it
is my right to tell you that ; but because I
do tell you, that is no reason why you
should shut up your voice in a box, and
only let it out through one tiny hole.
Come here, close to the light—stand—so
—that will do. I want to look at you."

And he did. He looked at me from
head to foot ; he measured my inches with
his eye ; he mentally criticized my figure,
which must, in comparison to his, have

seemed about as slight as a slate-pencil; he gazed thoughtfully at my face; with his hand under my chin, he examined my features closely; and then with a sigh he patted my shoulder, and said, sadly—

"No; it would be a waste of power and time. For that a woman must have a presence, or she must have piquancy. If diminutive, she should be bright, and arch, and pert, and coquettish. At the bottom of that sort of success there is always a devil, and thou hast no devil, Annie. If we could put one into thee, all might be different. Bah! what a stupid head I am to babble such folly! Let us go out and have a walk in this delightful air. Let us forget music and the world, and fancy we are back in happy Alford once again."

As we paced along, the fresh sea-breeze blowing in our faces, Herr Droigel, anxious apparently to dissipate that feeling of restraint which a pupil always, I think, feels towards a teacher, and which increases instead of decreasing as time goes by, exerted himself to amuse and interest me.

He could talk well when he thought fit to drop his absurd mannerisms and to discourse like an ordinary human being, and he chose on that day to speak about subjects which had a great fascination for me.

He told me concerning his youth; he described his birthplace; we lingered together in foreign cathedrals; he had much to say about the celebrated men and women with whom he had come in contact.

Never did I enjoy a walk more, and I was telling him so while we slowly climbed the hill on the top of which our cottage stood perched, when a small pony-chaise containing two persons, a lady and a gentleman, passed us.

Something in the lady's face seemed familiar to me. Something in mine apparently was familiar to her, for she said to her companion, without in the least lowering her tone—

"Stop the pony, George, and let those people overtake us. I think I know the girl;" and turning round she stared at me fixedly for an instant before exclaiming, "Yes, it is little Trenet. What in the world are you doing here?" And jumping to the ground she took both my hands in hers, saying at the same time, "You have forgotten me; you cannot remember who I am."

"I have not forgotten you, Miss Cleeves," I answered; "you are not changed in the least!"

CHAPTER IX.

OUTFLANKED.

A ND you," retorted Miss Cleeves, "are not altered one atom. I do not believe you have grown an inch taller, and you are the same cold-blooded animal who used to sit on stones in the middle of the Love, looking like a limpet, all the while you were singing like a mermaid."

Hearing this polite speech, the gentleman she called George laughed, and Herr Droigel executed a faint "Ha, ha!" by way of second; and though the description of my former self conveyed in the young lady's sentence was far from flattering, I could not help joining in the general merriment.

"Come, you can laugh, that is a blessing," remarked Miss Cleeves ; "and, as it is an accomplishment of recent date, I must inquire who taught it to you. Now, Annie, have you forgotten all your pretty manners, for which you used to win such praise in days gone by ? Do you intend to introduce me to this gentleman, or must I introduce myself ? Who is he—your guardian, or your husband, or both ?"

"Neither one nor the other," interposed the Professor ; "but Droigel, by adoption Miss Annie's father, and your most humble servant."

Miss Cleeves looked at him and at me sharply and curiously, then she said—

"Pray, Annie, how long is it since you discovered an adopted father necessary to your comfort and well-being ? You got on very well without either a real or sham parent, when I knew you. Or can it be," she suddenly added, "that this urbane gentleman is your step-grandpapa ? Has Mrs. Motfield——"

"That sainted and most God-loved woman—" Herr Droigel was beginning; but I could not endure the drift the conversation was taking.

"My grandmother is dead, Miss Cleeves," I said; "please, do not say anything more about her."

"Dead, little one! I am sorry," she exclaimed, and she put her arm round my neck. "George, take that ridiculous conveyance back to its owner, and leave me to find my own way to the Parade. I wish to discourse to this young lady about those 'days of auld lang syne, when we pu'd the gowans fine.' That is a dear fellow. *Au revoir.*"

And she kissed the tips of her fingers to her cavalier, who, turning a smiling and handsome face towards us, raised his hat, and, obedient to the word of command, drove off.

"And now, dear, tell me all about yourself," began Miss Cleeves. Then, ere I could reply by a word, she rattled on : " I have never been able to hear a sentence of you. My worthy relatives were dumb on the subject. Your uncle, whom I went to see, was ' obliged by the affection I professed and the interest I displayed,' but considered that as the 'ladies' objected to our intimacy, it had better cease. From that moment I have been a wanderer over the earth. I quarrelled with my bread-and-butter ; I flung it, as the children do, butter-side downwards, to the end that it may be good for nothing when picked up. I left the Great House, where, if everything was very slow, it was also very sure. My mother inherited a small fortune, and I went home to help her spend it. Then—well, then—she died"—with a glance at her black dress ; " and I am now with the Dacres—that is George Dacre," and she nodded her head after the driver of the departing phaeton. " We are all here for the benefit of the sea air and of sea-bathing. Between ourselves, I sometimes think Mrs. Dacre proposed coming here in the hope that I would drown myself; she is so dreadfully afraid of the son and heir marrying me— fancy that—marrying poor insignificant me!"

"And Mr. Sylvester," I asked, "where is he?"

"Oh, Sylvester is going to be Lord Chancellor, or something of that sort," she answered, with an uneasy laugh. "Fact is, little one, there never was in any respectable family such a kettle of fish boiled and served as that you prepared for our delectation when you left Lovedale. I denounced the conspiracy—I said things to Miss Wifforde, and Miss Wifforde said things to me, that were very much *comme il faut'n't;* and then—well, then—to cut a long story short, the original scheme had to be abandoned, and Mr. Syl left the Great House in order to make a name and some money for himself. He is still to inherit the place, I believe, if he behaves himself properly and turns out a good boy, and marries with the consent of his aunts. I always shall consider it a pity," went on Miss Cleeves, meditatively, "that I could not like him well enough to have a wedding. I am sure I shall some day do a great deal worse."

" Perhaps Miss does not know her own mind," suggested the Professor.

She looked up at him with a queer twinkle in her eyes, and answered—

"Yes, grandpapa Droigel, I know my own mind on that subject, at any rate. And now, you dear adopted parent of orphans like Annie and myself, tell me what you purpose making of this innocent. Has she still a voice, and does she intend uplifting it, or have you a son to whose Teutonic mind her *dot* does not seem simply contemptible ? Tell me, oh tell me, all about everything, ere I die!" and Miss Cleeves slipped her hand within his arm, and threw into her face an expression of the intensest interest.

"Miss Cleeves should go on the stage; she would make one actress so superb," remarked Herr Droigel.

"You charming man! repeat that observation," exclaimed the young lady. "Go on the stage! It is 'my dreaming by the night, my vision by the day—the very echo of my thoughts. My blessing'—et cetera. Go on the stage! I threaten my friends with that consummation; would to heaven I could only carry out my threat! Speak once more, dear friend—dear, if recent. Are you the Herr Droigel who writes those songs that fill one with rapture—that are a hundred, thousand, ten thousand times too spiritual and refined for the British public? Ah, no, it cannot be that I see you, of whom I have thought so often, at last in the flesh."

There are situations which prove irresistible; and to me the sight of Miss Cleeves standing in front of Herr Droigel, her hands clasped, her words coming thick and fast, and her eyes fastened on his ponderous person, as though it were the temple of some unknown god, was more than my gravity could withstand. Droigel himself accepted the position in the most perfect good faith, with the serenest amiability. Head uncovered, chest protruding, he stood there receiving Miss Cleeves's homage with an expression of such conscious worth, with a smile of such tolerant superiority, that at length, unable to control my merriment, I broke out into an almost hysterical fit of laughter.

"There you go once more, Miss Annie," said the Professor. "Who has held up a finger now before the baby, and said to her, 'Laugh, laugh at dat?'"

"I am very sorry——" I was beginning, when Miss Cleeves cut across my sentence.

"You are no such thing. You are, as you always were, a very ill-bred, ill-natured little monkey! Herr Droigel, let us leave her to enjoy the fun all alone. Do talk to me; tell me how you compose your songs.

Do they come to you in the night? do the waves whisper them to you?"

I heard no more. She was walking him up the hill as fast as her legs could carry her, and Droigel, who loved his ease, was toiling and trying vainly to edge in a word of remonstrance sideways.

As for me, I sat down on the grass, the short velvety grass covering the common land through which the road had been cut, and laughed till I cried, and then laughed again.

I had seen those songs written; I had beheld the throes of composition; I had heard all the saints in the calendar invoked and all the fiends adjured, when the melody born would not realize his conception of it. Often as not inspiration came to him just as a saucepan boiled or a favourite mess was placed upon the table.

"My child," he would then say, " one moment;" and the great hand would alight on the keys softly as a cat, and the mellow voice would hum a few bars, and thus a new air would come into the world, which was afterwards improved and elaborated till full grown and fit to be sent out into society.

When I reached the house, Miss Cleeves had already got Herr Droigel down to the piano.

"Hush-sh-sh!" she said, as I softly turned the handle and entered our sitting-room; "hush-sh-sh!" as though I had been in the habit of making riot and confusion wherever I appeared.

By the window stood Gretchen, puzzled; leaning against the instrument was Miss Cleeves, looking at the Professor as though she worshipped him.

When he had finished she drew a long breath.

"Ah," she said, "if I could sing, if I only could!" and she turned away, tears standing, I verily believe, in her eyes. "Herr Droigel," she went on, "I always feel religious when I listen to your music; how is that, I wonder?"

The composer professed himself unable to tell. Neither Gretchen nor I, had we been asked, could have afforded any assistance in the way of explanation.

"I want to hear you, Annie," she went on, after a pause. "I want to know if the voice has grown, or if it has got less, as I verily believe you have. You need not put on that sanctified and penitential look," she continued, "because——"

The good reason which no doubt Miss Cleeves intended to add was lost to us for ever, for at this juncture Herr Droigel rose and closed the piano with a careful silence, which spoke his intentions more eloquently than any bang could have done.

"You pardon me," he said, "but the dear friend of auld lang syne must not sing to-night; no—not for many nights. She is delicate, is this child, Annie; and when the good doctor, that devoted Packman, spoke to me of her, he said, ' It is a tender plant. If we wish it to blossom into perfect beauty, we must be careful to——' "

" And since what period of its existence has the plant developed such exceeding delicacy?" inquired Miss Cleeves. " To my ignorance she looks remarkably well. Fact is, I suppose, you do not want her to sing for me, and I must be content. There, am I not good and submissive and everything most proper and contemptible in woman ?"

" You are charming," said the Professor, bowing low. " Your words are in my ears like the sound of a wild melody—strange, yet delightful. Gretchen, my angel, Miss Cleeves has promised to do this poor abode so great honour as to eat and drink under its roof. Wilt thou take her to thy room, mine own, and procure for her what she may require? I hear the steady march of Ganymede carrying her tea-tray."

" And I hear the rattle of knives and

forks also, thank heaven!" added Miss Cleeves. "For your sake, Nannie, I have consented to forego the delights of dinner. Come with me, therefore, and make yourself amiable;" and she held out her hand.

I was crossing the room to join her, when Herr Droigel interposed. ·

"One moment, dear Miss. I have something so much particular to say to my child."

"Say it quickly, then," advised Miss Cleeves, "for I am going to wait till she is at liberty."

And she sat coolly down on a chair by the doorway; and taking off her bonnet, began swinging it backwards and forwards by the strings until our conference should have ended.

"Ah, ha! young lady, you are so droll," exclaimed Herr Droigel with a ponderous affectation of levity; "you wish to become acquainted with too much—you wish to know every one thing."

"I think I should soon know a great many things, Herr Professor, if I lived with you," said Miss Cleeves, calmly. "As I have not that inestimable advantage, I am waiting patiently till you have imparted valuable information to Annie. Now, you maker and singer of songs, what is it?"

"Every household has its little secrets," said Herr Droigel.

"Doubtless, and its big ones too; but I am certain any secret you may have to communicate to Annie can wait till 'with sorrow you see me depart.' Come, Annie, Herr Droigel is only practising on your credulity; he has no secret, my child;" and she swept me before her out of the room, and then turned and made a saucy little curtsey to the Professor.

"Ach, Heaven!" I heard him exclaim, "is she not adorable? Such piquancy— vivacity so great—coquette—born actress— inconceivable self-possession; but no voice —no voice; and that dear Annie——"

"Papa is composing a second book of Lamentations," remarked Gretchen, as she closed the door and ascended the stairs after us.

Miss Cleeves turned and looked at her, but said never a word.

No sooner, however, had we entered the apartment which we two girls shared, than turning to Miss Droigel, she began—

"Gretchen—I think your father called you Gretchen ; I believe he also called you an angel ; but parents are apt to entertain delusions concerning the attributes of their offspring — Gretchen, my angel, Annie Trenet and I have known each other since the days when, figuratively speaking, we sucked barley-sugar and made ourselves sick with gingerbread. Naturally there are many touching incidents we desire to recall, but we feel they are too sacred to be spoken of publicly. Therefore, Gretchen——"

"My dear Miss Cleeves," interrupted

Gretchen, seating herself on the side of the bed as coolly as the visitor had taken up her position below, " Annie is to us a very precious lamb, and we cannot run the slightest risk of having her morals contaminated. You see what a transparent innocent family we are ; we want to keep Annie as one of ourselves——"

" You will have to get her up to your own high standard of innocence first, girl with hair so golden and eyes so blue," said Miss Cleeves, cutting across her unfinished sentence ; " I understand the little scheme now, and in consideration of your father's inconceivable abilities will bow to his decision. I comprehend that this ' dear Annie,' to quote Herr Droigel, has developed the genius I first discovered ; and he fears that if her friends knew her real worth they might try to steal the diamond."

" Hardly, I think," said Gretchen, pillowing her ease-loving head upon soft round arms. "They would not know what to do with the diamond when they got it."

"Wise child of a wise parent," remarked Miss Cleeves, brushing her luxuriant hair with a quick impatient movement as she spoke. "Your words are words that I shall ponder upon. What an understanding there must be amongst this amiable family! Not a word spoken, and yet the youthful maiden knows her rôle as if by intuition."

"It is of no use trying to insult me," answered Gretchen lazily, yet defiantly, "I am but obeying orders. Annie's voice is precious to us; we want to make the most of it. So far the Droigels have been out of pocket over your, friend. In the future, the Droigels hope to enrich themselves through her. That is the solution of the enigma."

"You are frank, my friend," said Miss Cleeves.

"I am not false," retorted Gretchen,

angrily, answering not the words of the sentence, but the sneer it contained.

"You are fair," remarked Miss Cleeves, taking no notice whatever of Miss Droigel's indignation, "and I admire beauty. Farther, I confess that by your sublime coolness you have vanquished even me. It would not have hurt either your father or you to let me chat for five minutes alone with a girl I knew when she was so high; but as you think otherwise, I submit. Your uncle has sold you to the Egyptians, I see, Annie, and your friends must wait till you have achieved great renown before they behold your emancipation.—Let me know when the prodigy is to make her début, Miss Gretchen, and I will sell lots of tickets for you, and do that which is usually quite contrary to my principles—reward evil with good."

"You are very kind," observed Gretchen.

"I am not generally considered an amiable individual," replied Miss Cleeves.

"And now, Annie, you who were always a shuttlecock between contending battledores, and who will always be a shuttlecock till you develop a spirit and will and temper of your own, shall we go down to tea?— Heaven, what hair you have!" she went on, touching Gretchen's plaits almost caressingly. "I know it is rude to make personal remarks, but I never did see anything so beautiful."

To which compliment Gretchen made no reply, but stalked after us with uplifted chin and heightened colour, and a look in her eyes that said, It is of no use your trying to flatter and twist me round your finger. I am not a pliable idiot like our friend Annie.

As she had done ample justice to our fare at Lovedale, so Miss Cleeves delighted Herr Droigel's heart by the relish with which she partook of the various dainties displayed on the tea-table. Much must have been new and strange even to her, but, undaunted, she ate her way to my master's good opinion.

"Ah!" he said, *àpropos* to some observation made with Miss Cleeves's customary frankness on my appetite, " if Miss Annie would only take food, what a future might she not spread out before herself!"

" She was always a dainty little wretch," remarked Miss Cleeves, helping herself to a huge slice of German sausage.

"Don't you attend to the speaking of this dear friend," said Herr Droigel to me, evidently thinking Miss Cleeves's style of conversation calculated to wound my sensibilities; "she talks by contrary—she calls you 'wretch' for 'love.'"

" I beg you will not attempt to translate my language," answered Miss Cleeves; "Annie knows very well what I mean. Before she is fit to go out into the world and hold her own against the people that inhabit it, she will have to get rid of her absurd sensibility, of her extra refinement of sentiment, of her fastidious notions of gratitude and affection, and other rubbish of that sort. At this present moment she is just about as fit to steer her own course, and take care of her own interests, as I should be to command a man-of-war. If she had ten thousand a year it might be all very well, though even in that case somebody would make a fool of her; but for a girl who has to push her own way, who has, in a word, to earn her living, such trustfulness and want of self-assertion is simply ridiculous." And having thus delivered herself, Miss Cleeves asked for another cup of tea, whilst Herr Droigel stated his opinion that "gratitude and affection were traits most beautiful in the character of a youthful maiden."

"Beautiful, but useless;—worse than useless, pernicious," persisted Miss Cleeves; and then she began to laugh, and said, "Dear Herr Droigel, is it not fortunate for you that it is Annie with those traits in her character most beautiful, who has the divine voice, instead of a worldly-wise young lady like myself?"

" Who says Miss Annie has a divine voice?" asked the Professor, with an anxiety he tried vainly to conceal.

" I say so," replied Miss Cleeves. " What is the use of making a mystery about the matter? We all know the girl can sing; that she could sing from the time she could speak. You are as well aware of that as I am."

" Pardon me. Miss Annie is very dear to me; but of her voice I say nothing except this, that voices do not always grow. That which is wonderful in a child is weak in a woman. As she sang when I first heard her, our Annie sings not now."

" Then you must have made some terrible mess over your teaching," said Miss Cleeves, bluntly. For a wonder she did not perceive the equivoque of Herr Droigel's sentence; but I did, and exclaimed—

" No pupil ever pleased a master, Miss Cleeves. Put me on that stone in the middle of the Love with you for audience, and I will sing better than ever I did."

" A miracle," cried Miss Cleeves ; " the dumb speaks !" Then glancing slyly at Herr Droigel, she added, " It is a remarkable fact that the dumb always speak at the wrong time."

" Annie could never speak at a wrong time for me," said the Professor ; " that dear child has only two faults—she eat too little, she talk too little."

" I am not sure that talking too little is a fault," disagreed Miss Cleeves. " Supposing every one talked as much as you and I—why the world would be a perfect Babel."

" I, dear Miss !" expostulated the Professor ; " I—why, I am the most silent amongst men. If I had but your gift, I might then open my mouth. Then I could talk worth hearing !"

"Madame Droigel will be jealous if you compliment me," said Miss Cleeves, calmly. "She is aware that when I came here, I was in love with the composer; when I leave, I shall have to make the sad confession that I am in love with the man."

Madame Droigel laughed. "I am so mooch used to dat," she remarked; "the ladies are most in lofe with him. He is so goot to all."

"Thou flatterest, dearest one," said Herr Droigel, while Miss Cleeves turned upon me a look which was unhappily intercepted by Gretchen.

"I at least do not flatter," said Miss Cleeves. "Seriously I do not know a modern composer whose songs stir my heart like those of Herr Droigel; and farther, I always feel a respect for any one possessed of sense enough and will enough to outmatch me. You and your charming daughter have beaten me to-day. I did want half an hour's quiet talk with Annie; but you and she said ' No,' and I am forced to bow to your decision."

" What an intelligence !" exclaimed the Professor, lifting his hand as though asking Heaven to join in his admiration of our visitor. " Of what avail are the clumsy devices of a novice like myself when pitted against an intuition so rare, a sense so subtle ? Dear Miss, of what use beating about the bush with you ? I will show you my soul. I will speak to you about this dear child Annie as if she was not present. Lovely is the affection of woman, touching are the little confidences of the sex ; but they are too stimulating for constitutions like that of my Annie. Her mental digestion, so to speak, is weak. Sentiment overweights her. The tender memories of that childhood, so calm, so beautiful, are better to lie slumbering. She is excitable, this little one. If she is to do any good for herself, or for her devoted Droigel, she must keep tranquil."

"So far as I am concerned, I have no objection to her keeping tranquil," said Miss Cleeves. "The only stipulation I make is, that when she sings in public for the first time you give me due notice, that I may be there to hear."

"It is a compact," said Droigel.

"Let us shake hands on it then," suggested Miss Cleeves.

And the pair went gravely through this ceremony, after which Miss Cleeves remarked that it was time for her to be returning to the domestic hearth.

"I myself will have the great honour and pleasure of accompanying you," said Herr Droigel; and fortified by this assurance of safe escort, Miss Cleeves went upstairs to put on her bonnet.

I did not offer to go with her. If Gretchen was to remain as a spy upon me, Gretchen might do the honours of her father's house. Sulkiness was not a conspicuous trait in my character, but that evening I confess I felt sullen and aggrieved. For years I had worn fetters unconsciously; the moment I recognised their existence, I rebelled at my bondage.

Evidently Miss Cleeves guessed at what was passing in my mind, for as she kissed me at parting, she whispered, " I will see you alone in spite of them."

Equally certain was it that Herr Droigel knew I was out of temper, for he patted my head and called me his dear child, and bade me take care of myself till he returned.

As for Gretchen, scarcely was Miss Cleeves well outside the doors before she opened her battery.

" Are all your friends like that ?" she inquired.

" I do not know. Why?" I said, vaguely.

" Because, if they are, I cannot congratulate you on your acquaintance. Of all the ill-bred, insolent, rude, disagreeable people I ever met, that Miss Cleeves is the most unendurable. If she be a specimen of the upper ten thousand, deliver me from them!"

"I do not know anything of the upper ten thousand," was my answer; "but I suppose there are some of all sorts amongst them, as in our own rank."

"What business has she interfering with you?" continued Gretchen. "What does she mean by sneering at my father?"

"I do not think she sneered at your father. If there be anything in the world Miss Cleeves admires, it is genius; if there be anything she likes, it is a character out of the common; and Herr Droigel has genius, and he is not in the least like anybody else that I ever knew."

"Did she suppose I was such an idiot as to be deluded by her compliments? What can it signify to her whether I am pretty or ugly? I daresay she thinks herself far better-looking than I am."

"I do not know. If she entertained

such an opinion, I imagine she would have expressed it."

" Because you know she is pretty," went on Gretchen, anxious for contradiction.

" I think her beautiful," was my reply.

" I do not know about that," said the German Venus, disappointed ; " she certainly has a quantity of nice dark hair, and good eyes, and——"

" Do not let us dissect her, Gretchen," I said, gently. " You do not know exactly what she is to me—all I have felt about her since the first morning we met. Oh, if you could only see the place where she lived then !"

" Was it very grand ?"

" Yes, magnificent," I answered, in perfect good faith. Everything is comparative, and the Great House still seemed magnificent to me.

" Is Miss Cleeves very rich ?"

" No, I think not ; I do not know. She

might have been, if she would have married as Miss Wifforde wished."

"Why didn't she marry, then ?"

"Really, Gretchen, it is impossible for me to say."

"Did you ever see the 'him ?' Was he old, was he ugly, was he ill-natured ?"

"No, he was young and good-looking, and a vast deal better tempered than she."

"Then why on earth didn't she marry him ?"

"I have not an idea. And now, if there is no other question you particularly want answered, I wish you would leave me alone."

•Having uttered this polite speech, I walked into the drawing-room and locked the door after me.

"Sociable one," screamed Gretchen to me through the keyhole a few minutes after, "mamma and I are going for a walk in the moonlight—will you come ?"

"No," I said shortly.

" Well, you might be civil, at any rate."

" Do go for your walk, and never mind me."

" I hope you will be in a more amiable temper when we come back."

" I made no reply—I opened the piano and began playing.

" You are going to exorcise the demon, is it not so ?" persisted Gretchen. But I drowned her farther utterances with a crash of chords, and finally she departed. Then once again I had the house to myself, then once again I could sing.

Not, however, as had been the case in the earlier part of the day. As I played, my irritation vanished. The demon, as Gretchen surmised, was cast out by the music, and tender thoughts and gentle memories came swelling up in my heart, as I recalled Lovedale and the happy days I had spent there—the happy, happy days of old.

Forgotten melodies recurred to me : ballads that had lulled me to sleep; songs that I had heard crooned in the hay and the harvest-fields crowded back to my memory—unconsciously, almost, airs wild and plaintive took shape and form once more. With the bright moonlight flooding the room, I sang, in my girlhood, the songs of my earliest youth.

At this moment, moonlight " deep and tender " is lying calm, soft, and silvery over lawn and garden, painting with unreal colours tree, and shrub, and flower; and as I write, that night, which held folded within itself the memory of so much of the past—the presentiment of so much of the future—returns in fancy once again, and is very present with me.

Long after Gretchen and her mother had come in from their walk, Herr Droigel reappeared, joyous, not to say merry.

" Where is my Annie," he said, " that I may talk to her of those friends so dear, so charming ?"

Yes; he had gone into the house of this Colonel Dacre. That adorable Miss would take no refusal. She had dragged him into a mansion grand as a palace, into the bosom of a family distinguished as royalty. The mamma Dacre was a marvel of matronly beauty; the papa looked himself a soldier; and there were two young lady Dacres— and a friend so sweet, so lovely—all so sweet, all so lovely—and three sons.

The sons, and the daughters, and the friend had only one fault: they imagined they could sing.

"Gott in Himmel!" and the Professor clenched his hands, and ground his teeth, and stamped on the carpet.

"And then," he went on, after a pause devoted to bitter memories of false notes and poor voices, "time anyhow, anyhow, but always wrong. And then they would have me to sing; and that dear impassioned Miss almost embraced me — me, Droigel. She is unprecedented; she is incomparable;

she speaks French, German, Spanish, Italian,
—each one like a native himself. Such
talent, such originality! And she is writing a book, she tells me. And then the
good Colonel would insist on my drinking
some of the wine of my own Rhineland.
Ah! that *was* wine which Miss brought to
me with her own hands, saying in her
pretty airy way, she had much regret there
were no leaves with which to crown me;
and they have invited us all to a picnic
party, and I—foolish Droigel that I am—
have promised that we will take ourselves
there. How say you, Annie? Will it not
be pleasant for you to see the dear friend
in all the unrestraint of holiday-making on
the sea?"

What answer I made to this is imma-
terial now, for we never went to that picnic; we never tried the effect of holiday-
making on the sea.

Next morning but one, Herr Droigel
received, or said he received, a letter from

some wonderful musical friend, which necessitated his leaving for London and carrying me with him.

We only remained there long enough to enable his friend to hear me sing one " little song :" after which we parted in all haste, and started, he and I alone together, for the Continent.

Never a pleasanter companion need youth have desired than Herr Droigel proved himself; and yet I failed to enjoy my trip as much as would have been the case had I not entertained a strong suspicion that the journey was undertaken with no other object than to separate me from friends old or new.

One phrase used by Miss Cleeves perpetually recurred to me. Yes, I felt I was a shuttlecock, and that Herr Droigel was playing at battledore with me all by himself.

CHAPTER X.

A SLIGHT REMINISCENCE.

BELIEVING as he did in his "heart of hearts" that there was but one country worth speaking about, and only one people possessing brains, character, and romance—the Germans—it was natural that Herr Droigel should extol that "dear Albion," and even profess that, spite of its fogs, its prejudices, its shams, and its luxurious style of living, he preferred it even to the beloved Fatherland.

"After all, Annie," he said, as we approached London, "the song is right, there is no place like home, be it ever so lowly."

"But surely," I said, "you do not consider England home?"

"And why not, I pray you, little wise-head?" he inquired.

"Because it is not your home; because you are a German; because England can only seem to you like an inn, where you would never think of remaining for the whole of your life."

"Who is it that says he always found his warmest welcome at an inn? There, never mind racking your young brains over the matter. He was a wise man, and, I doubt not, a good, or he never would have arrived at a conclusion so full of profound sense and delicate feeling. To return to your question, let me answer it by another, Where is your home?"

"Oh, Herr Droigel," I answered, "I never had but one home. I never can have another."

"Your castle on the Love?" he suggested.

"Do not laugh at me," I said; "do not turn that home into ridicule. It was but

an atom of a place, it was absurdly small;
beside the Great House it looked a mere
speck; and yet I loved that home as I can
never love another so long as I live."

Herr Droigel lifted his hat; he put on a
solemn expression as if he were entering a
church; he looked at me with tender pity,
and then he began addressing vacancy, as
though I had been a subject, and he lectur-
ing upon me.

"What a child of nature is this dear
Annie! Her instincts, are they not those
of the faithful animals, who, being dumb
and without reason, rise superior to self-
interest and to deceit? Behold a house
desolate, its master dead, its mistress far
distant, its children scattered, its servants
disbanded; silent are its rooms, grass-
grown its gardens, across deserted apart-
ments the moon throws her ghost-like rays.
And by the lonely hearth, where no fire
now is lighted, where dust and ashes alone
remain to tell of the fires that once have

been, what do we behold ? A cat, with rough coat and staring eyes, the only creature that remains faithful to the memory of the past. Or see, once more, a grave in which man has been laid by man to rest till the judgment-day, or till some fresh tenant has need of the slender plot. Man has left man ; he has gone back to his pleasure, his business, his care, his money-making, his money-spending ; and the friend of old, the boon companion, the true comrade, the worthy citizen, the husband and son and father, exemplary in each relation of life, out of sight is fast growing also out of mind, and lies under his clay mound, with rank grass growing to right and left, at head and foot, alone. And yet not alone : stretched full length on the mound is the one friend whom death has failed to alienate —his dog."

Here Herr Droigel puffed forth a sigh, and remained silent for a moment—whether engrossed in the contemplation of cat or dog his own consciousness had evolved, it is impossible for me to say. When he took up his parable again, it was but to apply its moral.

" And as the cat and the dog in their attachment to place and person, so is this Annie of ours. She beholds fresh places— she visits fine cities, she sees countries beautiful as dreams of fairyland—and still the true heart remains faithful to its first beloved—the cottage by the Love. Old friends pass away ; the grandmother, so good, so tender, has long received her message, and repaired herself to the mansions of the blessed ; and other friends have arisen to help Annie along the path of life ; but Annie, devoted like the dog, clings in memory to that grave across which the sunbeams glance through the branches of that memorable yew. It is lovely, and yet pitiful. Why were we created reasoning beings, if we permit instinct

to rule our feelings and influence our actions?"

Herr Droigel's philosophy had become
wearisome to me in the course of time—as
wearisome as his sentiment; and for this
reason, casting aside the question whether,
in my divine instincts, I resembled his
ideal cat and dog, I returned to the point
whence we had started.

"You cannot," I persisted, "like England
so well as your own country."

"Mine own child," said the Professor,
"when the frosty weather nips you up—
soh!"—and he convulsed his mighty frame
with a stage shudder—"which do you
love best, a full grate or an empty? When
you are hungry—but hunger, I suppose, is
a sensation unknown to Annie, who nibbles,
nibbles, unlike Droigel, who eats plates
upheaped—but put it that you felt hunger, should you not prefer a larder well
garnished, to one empty and swept clean?
The royal sirloin, the substantial side of

bacon, the appetizing sausage, and the useful loaf would recommend their presence. Good; so far you follow me. This England of yours, cursed in its climate and—well, in nothing else, we will say—blessed in its soil and its wealth and its position, its blazing coals, is bread and meat, board, lodging, and washing to me. I find not here ethereal blessings—I find no appreciative public, no wreaths, no garlands, no medals; but in lieu thereof the cakes and ale which in my own land of poesy and romance might well be forgotten.

"Setting aside the fact of its being poisonous, a man cannot live on laurel. He needs the fat beeves, he delights in the fine wheaten bread with which London can supply him. It is true, and pity it is, that as regards Art the English are outer barbarians; but what matter? They know how to live, they know how to let live. There, Annie, much beloved, is the case in a nutshell, as your adage has it. A time there was—why should I, who wear my heart on my sleeve, seek to conceal anything?—a time there was when I, like you, had my aspirations. Just as you have often said in your innocent soul, 'When I have gained fame, when I have made money, I will steal back to the home that mine heart sickens for,' so, in similar manner, Annie, I have spoken to myself in my foolishness, and said—

" 'I will endure these fogs so fearful; I will humour the Goths, and write down to please the false taste and tickle the diseased palates of the Visigoths; I will haste me to be rich, and then return to mine own romantic land, and under the shadow of my vine and my fig-tree spend the remainder of my days.'

" But money is about the only evil not to be acquired with rapidity; and here am I fast hurrying down the hill of life, poor as when I first began to climb it. Yes, it has been a lost existence," finished Herr Droigel,

and his voice sank almost into a whisper.
For a moment, perhaps, he deluded his
fancy with the idea that circumstances and
not himself were to blame for the result of
his endeavours—that, given the chance
over again, the end would not have proved
such an utter failure as I must confess it
seemed to me.

"I was always a simpleton," he recommenced, after a pause; "the artist cannot
help being one, out of his art. The one side
of the artist's temperament is genius, the
other folly. Looking back—thinking about
what I am and what I might have been—
I say, 'Droigel, you were a fool, you are a
fool, you always will be a fool.' Then I
curse my folly, and at the first opportunity
am foolish again. Speak! is it not so,
Annie?"

Whatever my private impression of Herr
Droigel's character might be—and I am not
aware that I had then formed any impression at all on the subject—I certainly was

old enough and wise enough not to commit the impolicy of agreeing with his expressed opinions concerning his own imperfections; therefore, finding he waited for a reply, I said I thought he was so far from being a simpleton, that he could do anything he chose if he only liked to set about it.

"Ah! the sweet flattery of youth!" he exclaimed; "the only flattery which is honest and true! How dear is it to those who are young no longer! To a certain extent, however, you have reason, Annie. If I were other than I am; if, instead of being a child of nature, I were cold, calculating, worldly-wise; in a word, if Droigel were not Droigel, but another; then even now he might make a success. He might have his house large, well-appointed; his brougham snug and swift; his small boy covered with buttons tiny and bright; his coachman clad in a modest livery of drab and silver. But *ach nein!*" he suddenly exclaimed; "away, dreams! away, you mocking visions.

By the light of reason I see Droigel walking still through the mire of the filthy London streets, or else squeezed up in a close omnibus, anathematized by his eleven fellow-sufferers; no carriage, no high-stepping horses, no footmen, no nothing for Droigel till the end."

He was so pathetic in his self-pity that I could not possibly avoid trying to comfort him with the hope of brighter days in store; but my eloquence did not produce the effect it might, had imagination not conjured up a vision of Droigel settled down in a well-appointed house filled with decorous servants.

Would he clothe himself like other people? would he, could he relinquish his culinary occupations? What would a maid like Miss Hunter, for example, think of Madame's style of dress? and would not the necessary disorder of any abode which contained the Droigels fill with dismay the soul of any servant who ever took duster in hand?

"No, no, Annie," exclaimed my companion, "it is useless. I know what I know. The leopard cannot change his spots, and Droigel will be poor Droigel to the last page of the volume. The child of any other man than I would have been full of music, and Gretchen knows not one note from another. She cannot tell what is wrong or what is right. It is no sin to her. Music is a sense, and she has it not; but consider the difference to me. There was a little baby brother once. Was he crying and I struck a few chords, the tears ceased to flow." (Herr Droigel had evidently not studied the habits of babies so closely as the science of thorough bass, hence this figure of speech.) "At three years of age he could sing, in his dear little way, ballads to perfection. He was a prodigy, a wonder; but the angels took him. We have all our graves," added Herr Droigel with a reproachful glance at me, as though I had tried to monopolize the whole of them.

" Yes," he repeated, sinking his voice almost to a whisper, and communing apparently with his own absorbing sorrow, " we have all our graves."

A remark of this sort usually proves a dead-stop to conversation, and so it would in this case had ours been a conversation. But it was in truth almost a monologue, or rather, perhaps, a sermon preached to one auditor, a lecture delivered to a single listener. Having a good listener, Herr Droigel, after a moment devoted to sentiment, proceeded—

" Yes, it has been a lost life ; and no one to thank for it but mine own idiotic self. Knowing what was best, I did what was worst. I never looked ahead ; I thought wise thoughts and acted unwise deeds, like other men. There was my marriage, for instance. I ought never to have married, or at least not then. You need not look so frightened, Miss Annie ; I adore Madame Droigel, as you know."

"Yes," I answered, relieved, "I know you do." Many a time had I marvelled to myself how Herr Droigel could marry such a woman as Madame, and it did surprise and almost frighten me to hear him touch the string I had so often tried to sound when alone.

My knowledge of mankind was at that period extremely slight, and I happened to be utterly ignorant of the astonishing fact that many men consider it a delicate way of ingratiating themselves with the other sex, to state or imply that they have matrimonially made the wrong selection; but even had I then been aware of this singular masculine propensity, I could not have felt more alarmed at the idea of Herr Droigel suddenly going mad and making love to me, than I did at the notion of his selecting me for a confidant.

The only married man with whom I had any previous acquaintance was my uncle Isaac; and though his choice seemed to me as mistaken a one as imagination could conceive, still I knew no human being would ever hear from his lips confirmation of the theory.

For these reasons had Herr Droigel struck me a blow, I do not think I could have felt more utterly stunned than I was by his remark.

Calmly, however, he proceeded to reassure me. According to him Madame Droigel was the personification to his mind of female excellence.

" To you who know her," he said, " why need I dwell on her perfections ? She is, you must confess it, unique ; is it not so, Annie ?"

Happy was I that he had found a point on which I could agree with him so thoroughly. Yes, Madame was unique.

With tears in his eyes Herr Droigel thanked me for my divine appreciation.

" I knew you, so good, so amiable, must recognise those qualities in another. Think,

Annie, since you became our second daughter, have you ever seen her temper once ruffled ?"

" No, I never have." I was still with him.

" And then what adorable forgetfulness of self ! Other women might say, ' I must have this, I must have that ;' but my dear wife has no thought save for her most unworthy husband. Is it not inexplicable and touching ?"

To which I replied that I supposed any one who knew him would be only too happy to study his wishes ; but that still it was very nice of Madame to be so entirely devoted to his interests. Whereupon he smiled pleasantly, and said I was a little Jesuit.

" And still, through all your pretty speeches, underneath your simple innocent manner, I see you are dying to know why I say it was a mistake for me to marry any one, more especially a woman so far, far too good for me as that angel who bears with me as her husband. I will tell you. The artist should never marry. His art should be to him father, mother, brother, sister, wife, child, friend. When he is created into this world he is to all intents married already. If he takes to himself a second wife, he commits bigamy; for, look you, the art never dies until the man does. He may think he has seen its last breath, that for him its last sigh has been uttered; but it will come to life again. In an hour when the man or the woman least look for its appearance it will come to claim its own again.

"A man cannot serve two masters," went on Herr Droigel after a pause, during the continuance of which I never attempted to speak. "'He cannot love God and Mammon.'" (Under which category he intended to include Madame I have not the faintest idea.) "To one or the other he must be unfaithful. The wife goes to the wall, which is a wickedness that ought not to be allowed to happen, or the beloved art is neglected, debased into a mere device for money-making. No; the artist should be free to devote himself, body, soul, spirit, to his mistress—so beautiful, so exacting; so generous if served faithfully; so revengeful if another be placed upon her pedestal. From his cradle he who is born with genius should be taught that the delights of earthly love are not for him. He should have no children crying out for bread, while he is treading the pathway to Fame. In my poor way," he went on, "what has my experience been? I have been forced to choose between my art and my family. Could I see the dear ones want merely because there was a future before me? Could I go on composing for a select posterity, whilst the men and women my contemporaries offered me gold to write some little nothing which should please their barbarous taste? Put yourself in my place, Annie ; try to fancy your little feet slipped into my great shoes, and then say, married, was it possible for me to cast aside all regard for my dear wife, for my beloved children, and compass success at the result of their tears, their privations ?"

To me there occurred only one possible answer to this inquiry : clearly, Herr Droigel, having elected to take Madame for better for worse, was bound to support her and his children ; and I said so.

Still there was no divergence in our opinions ; still I was able to agree with the views he advanced, only I could not imagine why he favoured me by advancing them at all, and at such length.

"What, then, Annie," he asked, "do you take to be the moral of all this ?"

"I suppose," I answered, "the moral is what you have already stated. You ought to have devoted yourself to art instead of to Madame Droigel."

"True, so far ; but there is a wider moral

which has been also expressed by me, and there is a particular moral which applies to you : no artist should marry. *You* should not marry."

"I have not the least thought of doing so," I answered, marvelling what on earth should have put such an idea into his head, for I knew no one who could possibly marry me. Dr. Packman was the only single man of my acquaintance, and he might also have been my grandfather.

"Of course not. Now you have not ; at the moment, no ; but the moment will come, and the lover with it. Then remember my words. Marriage is not for you. An artiste you were born, an artiste you have chosen to remain. You cannot be wife and artiste too. I have seen genius stifled, happiness destroyed, two made most miserable because people would not believe art and home to be incompatible one with the other. Do you believe, Annie, that the opinion I have expressed is true ?

Say, my child. Answer without reserve."

"I have no doubt you are quite right in
your opinion," I replied, sorrowfully. After
all, though a girl's thoughts may not be
running on marriage and lovers, there is
something mournful in hearing that never,
whether as girl or woman, is home to become a reality for her. Yet my small
knowledge of life confirmed the truth of
Herr Droigel's words.

At every turn had not music produced
an element of discord between me and
those I was most anxious to please? Had
I not been forced to smother my own incli-
nations in order to avoid grieving the only
parent I ever knew? Had not music driven
us from Lovedale—rendered return to Fairport impossible?

Yes, he was right. He sat watching me
while I came slowly and carefully to the
conclusion in my mind that I had already
uttered with my lips.

"Never give up your art for the sake of a husband," he went on, after a short silence. "Believe me, no man is worth the sacrifice. Oh, I have seen so much of it! I have known so many hearts broken, beheld such bitter tears shed; could tell of shipwreck so utter, so soul-rending, that if my Gretchen had genius, as she has beauty, I would rather see her in her shroud than in her bridal robes."

"You do not take a very cheerful view of a singer's life," I said, trying to speak lightly. "Surely there must be some exceptions to so sad a rule."

"You mean—I gather from your face rather than your words—that though so many are mismatched, yet some there must have been happily mated. I think not, unless the art was abandoned; for if two possessed of genius marry, they are never satisfied. The idea that there is a fellow somewhere on the face of the earth for every human soul is pretty, if you like, but it is

not true—at least, I think it is mere babble;
at all events, when the two souls meet they
are likely as not married already, having
grown impatient of long delay; and that is
bad—that is very bad; married souls ought
not to meet. Besides, it is often only fancy.
They are not the right souls at all; but
they persist sometimes in thinking they
are, and then a scandal arises, and afterwards they find out that the complementary
souls—shall we call them?—must still be
wandering about some place trying to get
paired. Bah! Upon the whole, I do not
think it a pretty fancy. It is uncomfor-
table, unsettled, a house on the sand.
What is your notion about it?"

"I have no notion," I answered; "but I
should not like my soul to consider it
necessary to go searching after its double;
and I imagine it would be extremely unpleasant to have another soul playing
through life at hide and seek with mine."

"That is mine own Annie's sentence once

more. She brightens up, she laughs, she
makes faces mentally at hobgoblins, and
defies them. She can be merry, though
we talk of serious subjects. Serious subjects must sometimes be spoken of. I cannot tell why it happens that one I knew
long, long ago has been in my thoughts
to-day. I knew her young, I heard her
sing when her voice gave promise, and again
when the promise had been fulfilled. She
was one of those of whom one says two
babies were born, and the voice was sent
to the wrong one; for she never looked as
though she ought to have had a voice, or
to be on the stage, or anywhere except in
a palace, perhaps, with everything grand
about her, and everybody waiting upon
her.

" She did not seem to have a morsel of
passion. The angels could not be sweeter,
colder, fairer than that young girl. She
could not act—she did not understand
what acting meant, and nobody could teach

her; but she could walk, and the way in which she crossed the stage always brought down the house. Then she curtseyed; night after night she swept her acknowledgments to the audience with a grace that produced thunders of applause. I close my eyes that have seen so much since those old days, and the blue eyes, the cloud of golden hair, the delicate complexion, the slight, lithe figure, the pure, saint-like expression, are present pleasures once more. Had I, Droigel, been asked to name the last woman I knew ever likely to have a history attached to her memory, I should have said—there, never mind who.

"She was making her fortune—and the fortunes of how many others might she not have made!—when a young gentleman, one of your great English families, fell— soh! over head and ears—in love. He was of a house and a race respectable to a marvel, honest, honourable. At her feet he laid all he had—his title—he was titled—

his fortune, himself. In a word, would she marry him ? In a word, she said, yes.

"That did not surprise me. His asking her did not surprise me. I suspected she had a hankering after the good things and great people of society. I fancied he seemed a big fish landed to her. I concluded her divine eyes, her seraphic expression, her charming locks had conquered him.

"'And you relinquish your profession without a sigh, Mademoiselle ?' I said, after offering, in my clumsy way, the best wishes I knew how to express. 'You leave your admirers inconsolable ; you depart for ever from a stage which may never behold your like again ?'

"'Yes, Droigel ; yes, yes, yes,' she answered, with a charming petulance. ' I am weary of my profession—so weary, I hope never to hear a note of music again. My admirers will console themselves before another season has passed, and I shall depart from a stage I feel thankful to leave for ever.'

" 'I was right, then,' I remarked. 'The voice angelic was sent by Heaven to another infant, but delivered ·by mistake to you.'

" Whereat she laughed, and asked me to explain ; and when I explained, she laughed still more.

" 'Dear Droigel,' she made reply, 'the same idea has occurred to me so often, so often, only I could never put it into words. You are right. Somewhere a youth or a maiden is living a wretched life because of the voice given in error to me. I ought never to have been a singer ; it is not my rôle in the least.'

" 'You think that of a grande madame will suit you better ?' I suggested.

" 'I mean to try,' she answered gaily. ' Come and see, Droigel, how I support my character.'

" 'Child,' I said, ' if you are really going

to try this new life, better leave the old entirely behind you. Between Droigel and Lady —— there is a gulf fixed; but if Mademoiselle ever wants anything in which Droigel can serve her, she has but to hold up her finger and say, " Come." '

" ' Dear friend!' was all she answered; and then she held out both her soft white hands to me, and I would have kissed them ; but she drew me towards her, and touched my cheek with her lips. I had known her when she was young, so young."

Herr Droigel paused. For once, I believe his emotion was sincere. Then he resumed—

" Time went by—one, two, three, four years—and Lady ——, the once admired singer, had settled down into private life, and was almost forgotten. With great persuasion, her husband had prevailed upon his family to receive her. She had been, like most geniuses, lowly born, and the fact of her having risen to notoriety by her marvellous voice, did not help to mend her position in a house the members of which were pious as they were proud. Consider that conjunction, Annie—pious and proud. To me it seems awful.

" All this while scandal passed her by— gossip left her name out of its records. Then, one fine morning came my lady to me.

" 'Droigel,' said she, ' I am weary of my life. I long for the old existence, for the clapping, the excitement, the audience, the orchestra, the bouquets. I must sing once more, once if it be only once, and you must manage it for me.'

" 'And my lord?' I ventured to remind her.

" 'Droigel,' she asked, ' are you going to stand my friend, or are you not ?'

" 'I hope I am, madame,' I answered ; and the good God knows I meant to be her true, true friend, though it all turned out so miserably.

" I went to my lord; I told him her

desire. In his set face, as he listened, I read the story of their married life, and his ultimatum did not therefore astonish me.

"'Lady —— might return to the stage if she pleased, on two conditions : one, that she resumed her maiden name ; another, that she agreed never to seek again to behold her children.'

"I tried to move him, but in vain. She could take her choice—her art or her home. She had rendered his home miserable enough. For her he had made sacrifices, he said, such as none could imagine, and now she forgot all that ; she wished to go and exhibit herself once more.

" That was his idea of the nature of an artiste's feelings. Well, but then none of us had ever thought she had the feelings of an artiste !

" The children gained his point. She went back to her home and her duty. She loved the babies ; oh, if ever there was maternal love, that woman had it. Let me hasten on. The opera season once more; big bills—Reappearance of Mademoiselle ——. The lessee has, &c. &c.

" My dear, you might have knocked me down with a feather. I rushed hither, thither: every one was asking; no one could tell. I went to my lord's town house; my lord was not in town. I ascertained by result of much trouble that my lord was not at any of his many mansions in the country; that he was not visiting the Dowager Lady his mother, or any of his other friends; but that he was gone abroad. No one could say where, and no one could say either when he would return.

" I tried to see Mademoiselle herself, in vain. I failed to procure even one glimpse except upon the stage. Yes—she re-appeared. Once more the divine voice, once more the superb walk. Again the curtsey, the grace whereof had almost become historical. A second time she appeared, and I heard her then also.

After which the papers stated she had been attacked by sudden illness, and would be unable to fulfil her engagement.

" So time went by. I could learn nothing reliable about her, till one night I was sent for suddenly to the house of a good and wise physician, and—but no, I will not tell you the tragedy which had occurred. Her husband was written for, and returned too late. She was dead when he came, happily for herself."

Whether Herr Droigel's reticence was induced by a desire to spare my feelings, or a consciousness that if he divulged the whole circumstances of the case, it might have spoiled the effect of his argument, I can only conjecture.

Certain it is, had I known then, as I knew afterwards, that the poor lady was insane when she returned to the stage ; that her mania, previously unsuspected, declared itself positively after her second appearance ; that she subsequently fell into a state of profound melancholy, and was placed under the care of that good and wise physician Herr Droigel mentioned; that the tragedy he referred to was the murder of her baby by the poor demented creature, I should stoutly have denied that at the door of either art or marriage so terrible a catastrophe could be laid; but I am not so certain now that my contradiction would have been right.

The life she had to lead in her husband's house was enough to kill any one who knew the meaning of the word "liberty." Cold though her nature was, small though her Bohemian proclivities were, still the bars of her golden cage must have broken the heart that beat in vain against them.

But of the true incidents of the lady's life I was then ignorant, and consequently Herr Droigel's narrative and conversation left me with three questions wandering through my mind, none of which I could answer.

What was the nature of the tragedy

that he so darkly indicated? Why had he, usually so reticent on such matters, introduced the subject of matrimony, and persisted in discussing the imprudence of art committing bigamy, to make use of his own idea? And third, who in the world could he imagine I should want to marry, or would wish to marry me?

CHAPTER XI.

HERR DROIGEL IS GRIEVED.

THE fact of Herr Droigel honouring me with his confidence was not the only surprise I experienced on my journey back to London.

"You love the country, Annie," he suggested. "The leaves and the flowers of summer, and the bare branches and dry twigs of winter."

"Yes," I answered, finding he paused for a reply; "I love the country at all times and in all seasons."

"You would like to live there continually."

"That would depend," I said.

"Upon what? You speak like an enigma."

"And you ask such singular questions," I retorted. "Of course I love the country, but I should not like to go back and live there always, unless I had first done something—made a success, or proved a failure," I added, wondering at my own boldness in pronouncing the last word.

"Less elegantly, but more epigrammatically,—'made a spoon or spoiled a horn,'" said my companion. "I understand what you mean. We have been playing at cross-purposes. When I spoke of 'country,' I had not in my thoughts a place similar to Alford, or even the beloved Lovedale, but a cot with its back door opening into London, and its front door affording access to green fields, to lanes so beautiful, to walks tranquil as a dream. How would such a habitation suit the tastes of romantic Annie?"

Romantic Annie, believing that the question was entirely a supposititious one, relating to some vaguely-intended change of residence at a future and indefinite period, replied that it would suit her tastes well.

"Then it is yours!" said Herr Droigel, clasping my hand between both of his, and turning up his eyes in an ecstacy. "We are flying there now! The country-bred bird will with delight enter into possession of her nest embosomed in ivy."

"What do you mean?" I asked. "Have you taken a new house?"

"Behold the divine common sense of the English nation exhibited even in the tender person of this unsophisticated child!" exclaimed Herr Droigel, addressing vacancy. "I talk poetry to her; I would have discoursed of honeysuckle, bowers, and nightingales; but she seizes my imagination, and with relentless grasp brings me back to the level ground of fact."

"There are no honeysuckles, leafy bowers, or nightingales now," I remarked.

"There will be, and I can see and hear and smell them," he replied. "I stand in the porch, and the scent of flowers floats to me in the calm evening air; I open my windows, and the roses put in their pretty fresh faces; I sit up at night to compose my poor songs, I lay down my pen, and there arises a burst of melody."

"Then you have taken a new house," I interrupted.

"Thou hast spoken, little maiden," he answered.

"Where is it?" I asked.

"Where is it? Let me think. As you stand under the dome of St. Paul's, it is north. How far north? You wish to know. Not far. Young feet with no care clogging their steps might walk to Westminster and feel little weariness. It is the typical cottage of happy England. It stands a little back from the road—the road, by the way, is a lane—sheltered from

vulgar gaze by high hedges of yew, thorn,
and privet. Fairy thorns, weeping wil-
lows, drooping ash-trees, stately evergreen
oaks stud the tidy lawn ; the porch is a
mass of honeysuckles, roses, and ivy —
the three strive together for mastery ; the
rooms are small, the rooms are low ; but
they open one into another, and so out
on to a garden, where southern breezes
woo the modest violets to bloom, and the
tender primroses to start into beauty.
Does the description please you, Annie,
my child ? Say, is it the modest ideal
crystallized ?"

I had not crystallized in my own mind
the question I wanted to ask concerning
this sudden change of residence, and so
remained silent, revolving the problem
unexpectedly presented, till Herr Droigel
inquired—

" Of what is the child thinking thus
earnestly, with bent brow and downcast
eye, and lips compressed ?"

"I was wondering," I answered, "whether you would be frank with me ?"

"Frank with you !" he exclaimed. "Am I not always frank to a fault ? open as the day ? Ask, and I reply, dear Annie. What hast thou in thy mind to say ?"

"I want to know why you have moved from London, and so suddenly."

"Explicit," he observed ; then proceeded : "Were I not frank, did I ever keep anything hidden behind the door of my thoughts, I should now give you a dozen reasons for the change, any one of which might be true, and yet keep back the truest of all. You see what a weapon it puts in your hands dealing with a man who has nothing in reserve, who, in matters of the world, is guileless as a baby. And you too, Annie, you are guileless ; but you are wise and prudent, and reasonable for your years. Listen to me. The time comes, say in another twelve months, when we must try, you and I, our little venture. We must take that first step which costs, and whenever or however it is taken, I want no one to have a foregone conclusion as to how it is likely to turn out. I have enemies. Who has not? There are those who could tear the flesh from off my bones, because I have composed a few songs that have become popular. Some, strange as it sounds, are even jealous of my small musical knowledge. They say 'Bah!' when Droigel is praised. When an audience is so good as to clap—as is the barbarian practice in England—and shout 'Encore!' they hiss, they cry 'Hush!' they shrug their shoulders. Now, if one of these heard I had a pupil with a promise, they would at once begin disparaging. They would exclaim, 'Pooh, pooh! we know Droigel's dreams of old. He has no sense, no understanding, he recognises not a voice when he hears it; he believes in voices which are not. This girl will make a fiasco.' And the

British critic — who himself comprehends nothing of music, and who forms the opinions of the British public, who comprehend less—will listen and be persuaded. He will write : ' The young lady's upper notes are reedy ; or her lower, rough ; or her middle, weak.'   Or he will say : ' She lacks expression, or her time is defective, or her ear false.' "

" What a prospect !" I remarked.

" It is nothing," said Herr Droigel ; " the poor man has his bread to earn, and we have ours.   It is my business to get the start of enemies and idiots.   It is for me to make at one stroke a *coup* which shall settle your position in the judgments of those whose judgments are worth having.   Besides, we shall want all the health and strength, all the energy and courage and faith the pure country air knows so well how to give.   A home by the murmuring sea might have been preferable, but I could not compass that, alas !   No."

" Then," said I, " you desire to take me a Sabbath-day's journey into the wilderness, solely that I may be beyond the reach of your enemies."

"Consequently yours; though they may not as yet be aware there is in existence a creature in every respect so admirable as our Annie."

" And not to render it impossible I should ever see any of my friends ?" I went on, ignoring the compliment contained in his reply. Compliments from Herr Droigel were to me fast becoming almost as valueless as pearls to swine.

" Who are your friends ?" he asked, without a trace of surprise. " Your good uncle, the adorable Packmans——"

" Say also, for the sake of argument, Miss Cleeves," I interrupted, foreseeing and dreading the adjectives which would be prefixed to the names of Madame, Gretchen, and himself.

"What !" he exclaimed, innocently; "that

Miss so piquante, so clever, so bewitching, who ate and drank with a naturalness and perseverance most commendable ; Miss who condescended to let me walk by her side to the house of her uncle ; Miss who did talk, talk, talk ; who has but one fault, that she is too clever ; Miss, so affectionate, so eccentric ! That Miss would not be your friend at this supreme crisis, Annie, but your enemy."

"And why ?" I asked.

"She loves you, but she has no sense in her love. She would speak of that as a certainty which is as yet but a hope. She would run hither, thither, saying to this one and to that, ' You must take tickets in order to hear my friend ; she sings like an angel ; I have known her since she was a baby ; she has the most wonderful voice in the world ; she has been instructed by that funny fat old Droigel ;' and so forth, and so forth, and so forth. And then her friends might be disappointed and say,

' Pooh, the girl is a nothing ; I wish I had
my money back that I was so foolish as to
pay for hearing a ballad I could have sung
better myself.' "

I have before said it would be vain to
attempt a reproduction in writing of Herr
Droigel's English, and it seems almost as
hopeless to describe by any word-descrip-
tion the manner in which he gesticulated
whilst delivering himself of the foregoing
sentence. He pulled his face into all sorts
of contortions, he shrugged his huge
shoulders, he mimicked Miss Cleeves'
voice and manner, he kept his hands
moving about as though on the key-board
of a piano to indicate the way in which
she would run hither and thither. He was
irresistibly funny, and for the life of me
I could not help laughing even while I
answered—

" But that is precisely what Miss Cleeves
will do, whether you keep me in solitary
confinement or not."

In a moment Herr Droigel was quiet, over his features there came an expression of touching melancholy.

"You should not have said that, child, dear to me as one of mine own; you should not hurt wantonly one who has been a friend to you—faithful, true."

"I am sure you have," I hastened to reply, "and I did not mean to hurt you. I did not mean the expression literally, of course. Pray forgive me, I am sorry to have vexed you."

And I was sorry, for the man had been kind and good to me; I was young too in those days, and young people do not, as a rule, like hurting the feelings of their elders. The tears stood in my eyes for very shame at thought of my petulance, and I stretched out both hands in token of repentance. Sadly and solemnly Herr Droigel accepted them and my submission.

"You are a good child, Annie, and very dear to me; but you are weak, and I have

my fears for your future. You never did, you
never do, walk straight on firm and fast
by reason of being quite sure where you
mean to go. You hear one say that the
road is full of dangers, you must not
attempt to travel it, and so you halt and
linger there ; then you go a little farther, and
another exclaims, 'You are not pursuing
the right path !' so you, like Christian in the
divine allegory of your Bunyan, turn aside
into field-paths through which you flounder
into Doubting Castle and the hands of that
special enemy of all of a hesitating temperament, the great Giant Despair. Then
one comes to you and takes you by the
hands, and talks to you softly, and offers
to put you in a way of reaching the goal,
and is quite determined to have care of
you by the road. He is able to fulfil the
promise made audible to the dear sensible
uncle, and silently and sacredly to his
own soul. In his own rough manner
he tries to make the adopted child happy,

good, successful. He pets, he scolds, he teaches, he entreats, he storms, till the voice which was once only sweet, becomes a marvel of flexibility and power; till success, if she will only take heed, is a certainty, not a possibility; and then behold what happens! The pupil so promising meets a Miss whom she knew for a day or two years ago, who never did her anything but mischief, whose proud relations drove the beloved grandmother to seek in her declining years a strange home in a strange place, and in a moment she begins to doubt again, she wants to go off hand in hand with the clever demoiselle; she would ruin her chances, she would go here, there, everywhere, she would sing to any one, she whose notes are precious; and because Droigel puts down his foot and says no, the poor silly little *mädchen* huffs, pouts, frets, and is very much inclined to quarrel with one of the few real friends she has in this wide, cold world."

"It is not so, Herr Droigel," I answered, when at length the wordy torrent moderated. "I confess I have been out of temper, but not for the reason you state. I know you have taught me all I am able to do. I know you have spared no pains to make me a singer; I daresay you understand what is good for me much better than I do myself, and I am quite ready to do anything you tell me if you only explain why you desire it; if—if only you will not treat me like a child."

"And, mein Gott," ejaculated Herr Droigel, turning up his eyes and invoking some deity included in his own theology, and of which certainly no recognised creed had knowledge, "what are you but a child? Suppose for the sake of talking babble, I say when we arrive in London, 'Good-bye, sweet one; we part here, big Droigel and little Annie;' what would you do?"

"I cannot tell," I replied; "but that is nothing to the point, for most women

would not know what to do if left suddenly
alone in a great town where they have only
lived in one house, the door of which is
shut upon them.   I am not a child, and it
makes me cross to be treated like one.
There, Herr Professor, you have had your
say, and I have had mine."

"Oh, these women," he murmured, softly,
"these children !"

"These men !" I added, laughing.

"You are a naughty girl," he remarked ;
"but Droigel cannot be unforgiving to his
youngest, to the Benjamin of his age.   You
are a child no longer, you say, and—well,
to please you we will cede the point.   What
does Annie the woman want ?"

"She wants you to treat her as you
would a woman," I began—here Herr
Droigel cast a look upon me which was at
once a mixture of amusement and compas-
sion—"not to humour and deceive her as
you might a baby."

" Go on, I listen to you," he said ; " condescend to explain."

" For instance," I proceeded, " had you told me your views concerning Miss Cleeves, I should have written to let her know exactly how matters stood."

" Go on," he repeated ; " I listen, I admire. Oh, the tact so divine of this English people !"

" There was no need to make a mystery about it," I continued, boldly ; " there was no necessity to go abroad."

" How grateful is this English people !" he interrupted ; " they deserve to be—rich."

" I hope I am not ungrateful," I said ; " I have had a delightful trip—I never enjoyed anything so much in all my life as I did our journey ; but still, had you said one word to me, only one, that evening Miss Cleeves spent with us——"

" Enough," he said, as I paused, really not knowing how to proceed—" enough !

I think I comprehend the intricacies of your heart now. To spare you trouble, to keep the bloom on the peach, the dew on the rose, the green leaves over the sweet violet, I have held you in ignorance of some few whys and wherefores. You want all that swept away; you would have the veil of mist which intervenes between youth and reality dispelled; you want to look out through plate-glass on a world which has some ugly corners; you want nothing softened, nothing concealed; you want me, to use your imperfect English expression—*gauche*, as all English expressions must of necessity prove—'to be frank with you.'"

"If you can," I answered, eagerly. I did not mean to be rude, but the sentence slipped out unawares.

Herr Droigel seized hold of it, however.

"It is for this we rear children," he said, addressing that imaginary audience he always seemed able to conjure up before his mind at a moment's notice. "It is for this we wake when others sleep; for this we rise early, and take rest late; for this we eat the bread of carefulness."

"For what?" I inquired, though I knew without his telling me.

"For ingratitude which is keener than a serpent's tooth," he answered.

"I am not ungrateful, I hope," I said for the second time. "I know all you have done for me. I have always been, and I hope always shall be, ready to acknowledge that I owe every atom of learning I possess to you; that you and Madame and Gretchen have been good and kind to me; that I have been happy ever since I came to London; but you have not been frank with me."

"Not been frank with you! Well, it is of no use reasoning with one of your divine sex—no, not from the time she is in long clothes. Have your own way, my dear, and your own opinion. You will have both, whether I say yea or whether I say nay. You want to see not merely my actions, but to scrutinize my reasons for them. You want to peep here and there, like every other woman, if there is a closed door, and you are told there is nothing on the other side of it. You want, in a word, to see nothing. There is nothing hidden in me, child of my heart, whose petulance I forgive. You might look down, down into Droigel as through the waters of a clear lake; nothing lies at the bottom of his nature except a desire to spare pain, trouble, and anxiety to those who are more to him than himself. He has no Bluebeard chamber; but though there is nothing in the whole of his house worth seeing, you shall be made free of it. I say to you from this hour, Annie, take the keys and see whether there be any disguise, any secrecy, any of your English reserve, at once so repelling and so suspicious, about the foolish old dotard, who, cruel and unjust as she is to him, loves the orphan he found weeping under the shadow of a grey tower in a graveyard so quiet, so still, so beautiful, so sad."

When he mentioned those keys which were to unlock the chambers of his heart, Herr Droigel took my hand in his and made a feint of putting the magic present into it.

What could one do with such a man, except look amiable again after having looked sulky? If you tell a friend he has a smut on his face, and the friend persists the black exists only in your imagination, has been created solely by your deficiency of vision, of what avail is remonstrance or iteration? He will not believe, and there is not the slightest use in trying to make him believe.

I had drawn a shade across his transparency—that was the way in which he subsequently alluded to our conversation—but the darkness came from my nature, which though most "lofeable," was still

English and eccentric.   Droigel's mind was
"incapable of casting a shadow."

"Is it not so, mine Annie?" he said,
when, I having, as usual, given way on
every particular, we made up our little dis-
agreement and were friends again. "Did
you not view the faithful adopted father
through the medium of a cloud of British
spleen? Have I ever had any secret from
you which it behoved you to know? Am
I not clear as the day?"

"That goes without saying," I answered,
weary of the controversy.

CHAPTER XII.

OUR INVITATION.

THE change to the suburbs was in many respects pleasant; and though we went to our new abode at a season when the worst part of the year for town or country is coming on, still to me the face of the country seemed that of an old friend.

After all, the hollies and the laurels, the evergreen oaks and the yew-trees, were better objects on which to rest one's eyes than the backs and fronts of other houses. It was agreeable, also, to sit in the pleasant pretty drawing-room, with the French windows open, singing to one's heart's content with never a soul to hear, and the rain pattering on the verandah

by way of accompaniment to the piano.
The kitchens were well away from the
living rooms ; and in them Madame always
—and Herr Droigel when at home—spent
much time. More ineffably nasty dishes,
more indescribably curious *plats* were, I
think, concocted in Woodbine Cottage—so
our new abode was called—than had been
the case in the heart of London. We
boasted a garden well stocked with herbs
and such vegetables as furnish variety in
autumn and early and mid-winter, and
amongst these the Professor browsed like
an ox turned out into fresh pastures.
Never before probably had he revelled
amid such a profusion of good things as
were contained in that kitchen garden.
Good heavens, in what startling combina-
tions he rejoiced ! Sweet he made bitter ;
bitter he made sweet. He stewed cabbage,
he served up broccoli with sauces, the very
aroma of which was an offence to my
nostrils. Savoury herbs pervaded every

morsel we put into our lips. He divided his leisure between the kitchen and the garden, between the range and the green-house. He exhausted his knowledge of English in adjuring a new maid-of-all-work and delivering lectures to the gardener—whom I once overheard muttering that "the old cuss always kep' a-messing and a-talking and a-poking his inquisitive nose into places that warn't no bisness of hisn."

If it had ever entered into the mind of this gardener that a suitable selection of vegetables might be made from our stock and devoted to his own use or that of a friendly greengrocer between whom and himself pecuniary arrangements stood on a proper footing, he must have been a miserably disappointed man; for I think not the value of a sprig of parsley escaped the Professor's watchful eye. Keen as was his ear for music, I think his sense of possession was keener still.

We ate vegetables "like cows," I understood was the gardener's unflattering
comment passed upon the whole of
us; "and as for salads, large and small,
they might be rabbits theirselves, they
might."

Had Herr Droigel been an Englishman
he must have succumbed to that gardener.
As it was, the gardener struck his colours
at the end of a month. He couldn't stand
it, and he wouldn't; and he didn't, for he
went; and as we did not entreat his return, revenged himself by writing to his
master, the owner of our furnished house,
that "Mr. Droggle" was ruining the place;
that he had already stripped the garden
clean; that he was turning the conservatory into a stove, and that every plant
would be roasted up alive; that we kept
no servant, and that everything was "going
to wrack and ruin;" that we lived like pigs
in a sty, and lived on made messes, slops,
and roots—all of which mass of information

was sent with the "duty of your humble servant, Robert Hayles."

Certainly Mr. Hayles never would have written such a succinct account of our shortcomings had he considered for a moment that it might bring his employer back from Devonshire, where he was wintering for the sake of a delicate wife.

His idea evidently was that Mr. Merrich would at once insist on his tenant resigning the reins of government to Robert Hayles, and so avert that acme of wreck and ruin so tersely indicated as coming upon his possessions.

Innocent of evil—for indeed we had but utilized for ourselves those vegetables which Robert Hayles considered ought to have been sold for the public good—we were, totally unaware of the threatened thunderbolt, one morning pursuing our accustomed avocations when Mr. Merrich arrived.

Madame was in the kitchen doing nothing,

as usual; our maid—a snuffy and rheumatic woman of threescore and ten—was in a very demi-toilette washing up the cups and saucers; Herr Droigel had gone to town; Gretchen was preparing for a purchasing expedition; I was trying a little air I turned up in an old music-book, exquisitely simple, and for that reason perhaps all the more difficult to learn to sing properly—

> " Komme, lieber Mai, und mache
> Die Bäume wieder grün,

I was beginning over again when Gretchen, looking handsomer than ever, and attired for walking, entered the room.

" What an idiotic air that is you are hammering away at, Annie!" she observed, with the freedom of criticism which lends such a charm to family intercourse. " I am quite weary of hearing you."

" You wont hear me when you are out of the house," I answered.

" No; and I hope you will have done

with it by the time I return," she retorted.
" Anything you want me to get for you?
Adieu, then; *au revoir!*" and she left me
to proceed with my studies.

Once more I began—

> " Komme, lieber Mai, und mache
> Die Bäume wieder grün,
> Und lass an dem Bache
> Die kleinen Vielchen blühn,
> Wie noch ich doch so gerne
> Ein Vielchen—"

At this juncture the door opened for the
second time, and Gretchen appeared, usher-
ing in a gentleman, who bowed as I rose
from the music-stool and glanced from him
to Gretchen with a vague alarm.

" Miss Trenet — Mr. Merrich," said
Gretchen, and I knew he was there on no
pleasant business; but even while I guessed
this vaguely, I understood that Gretchen's
beauty, and Gretchen's appearance, and
Gretchen's ready wit had averted the evil.

" Do you know when papa will be home,
Annie?" she went on; and then when I

said I did not, without giving Mr. Merrich time to make any observation, she left the apartment, remarking—

" If you kindly sit down for a moment, I will tell mamma you are here."

Left alone with our visitor I essayed conversation. I tried the weather; I made observations on the neighbouring scenery; I even ventured to hope that Mrs. Merrich had derived benefit from the change to Devonshire. Fresh also from continental travel, I found something to say in disparagement of the English climate.

On all these varied topics Mr. Merrich made civil though not encouraging comments; and I was racking my brains to find something more to say to him when he suddenly took the initiative.

" You are a relation of Herr Droigel, I presume ?" he began.

" Courage," thought I. " It is easier to answer questions than to originate conversation."

" No," I answered, aloud. " I am only a pupil."

" But you reside with the family, I presume ?"

" I have lived with Herr and Madame Droigel for several years."

" You must not think me impertinent for making such inquiries," he continued ; " but the fact is, I received a letter about my tenant which induced me to come up from Devonshire and see Herr Droigel. Of course I have only to look at this room" (Gretchen and I, proud of the pretty furniture, had decked it out with flowers and greenery) " to feel sure the whole of the statements which have been made are untrue ; but still——"

" I cannot imagine any statement made about Herr Droigel to his discredit," I replied bravely enough, though my heart began to beat fast, for somehow the idea of libel, whether true or false, affects one like a sudden blow. " I knew him first at the house of a valued friend, and he has been very kind to me; and I did not imagine until this moment that there was any one in the world who would speak ill of him."

"There was not very much ill spoken," answered Mr. Merrich, with a smile. "My correspondent only said the house was not properly cared for, and that the garden was in shocking order. You see I am quite frank about the matter."

"I do not think the house is in shocking order," I remarked. It would have been a shame if it had been, considering the pains Gretchen and I were at to keep it neat.

"Neither do I, Miss Trenet," he said with a smile, glancing round at the tables, vases, mirrors, and chairs his own money had bought.

"And as for the garden," I went on, "we were only three days without a man to attend to it. The person you employed left suddenly, and we were unable immediately to supply his place, but Herr Droigel saw to the conservatory himself; he is very fond of flowers; and there was nothing spoiled. Perhaps you would like to walk round and see?"

He hesitated for a moment, but then said straightforwardly—

"I am rather proud of my little place, and should not have let it to every one; so perhaps you will excuse me if I confess——"

"Were Herr Droigel at home," I interrupted, "he would insist, I know, upon your inspecting every nook and corner;" and wrapping a shawl round my shoulders, I stepped out upon the lawn, Mr. Merrich following.

We paced slowly round the walks; we visited the stable-yard; we loitered in the conservatory; and we became such friends that before we re-entered the house I had seen the letter, and understood we were indebted to Robert Hayles for the honour of Mr. Merrich's visit.

I could not help laughing over the gardener's statements, they were so true although they were so totally false; the whole epistle was such an admirable caricature of our establishment and ways of life, whilst at the same time it contained such an accurate reflection of Hayles' disappointment, that it was utterly impossible to read the epistle with gravity.

"I am unable to imagine, Miss Trenet, how you can derive amusement from such a scandalous production," remarked Mr. Merrich.

"He does not say anything very bad about us," I replied. "Gretchen and I have been laughing ever since we came here at the contest between Herr Droigel and your man. His habit evidently was formerly to provide what he chose for the kitchen. Herr Droigel's habit is to take what he likes; and we have had vegetables in every way vegetables could be cooked, except plainly, during the course of the

last few weeks. I shall not know a carrot
or a turnip if I ever see it dressed *au natural*
again. Here," I went on, "is the Professor's
stove. He has made himself a little forcing-
house in this corner for raising salads ; but
I do not think the place is going to 'wrack
and ruin' at present."

"Really, Miss Trenet, I am disgusted to
think I ever had such a fellow in my em-
ployment, and I feel utterly ashamed to
have for a moment given credence to his
slanders."

Presently Gretchen joined us. Softening
down the more grievous accusations brought
by Hayles against the Droigel family, I
told her he had represented we were fairly
stripping the grounds ; and she afforded us
considerable amusement by speculating how
her father would direct arbor-vitæ sprigs to
be served, or what sort of physical con-
dition we should be in after a stew of
laurel-leaves.

"She had been desired by her mother,"

she said, "to request Mr. Merrich to join us at luncheon." Gretchen had even then an eye to effect, and did not choose to call our midday repast dinner. "It would be a satisfaction," she remarked, "for him to have something out of his own garden before we finished the whole of its contents."

With the air of a man who felt he had been placed in a very false position, and who was determined to speak a few words of a disagreeable nature to his late employé, Mr. Merrich accepted the invitation, and we entered the dining-room, where Gretchen had with her own hands set out the table, and where we found Madame dressed in her best black-silk gown, a cap on her head, and her hair tidy.

"What a task I have had!" whispered Gretchen, and she made a *moue* expressive of the endurance of much mental anguish.

But it would not have mattered much what Madame had donned. Our land-

lord's eyes were too intently occupied with
Gretchen—who, fair and tall and graceful,
looked the very incarnation of a future
queen of song—for him to have leisure to
scrutinize very intently the appearance or
attire of any other person present.

"I suppose," he began after a time,
speaking in that stilted phraseology which
so many people think proper to adopt when
addressing a person who is a public character, or any embryo who is likely to become
so—"I suppose it was in your interest
Herr Droigel sought this retirement?"

"No," Gretchen answered, smiling; "I
think had he consulted either my interest
or my wishes, he would have remained in
town. I am not particularly fond of the
country, or its counterfeit the suburbs."

"Oh, I beg your pardon. I understood—that is, I imagined Herr Droigel
hinted something about quietness and
repose being necessary for perfect health
and voice."

20—2

"My health is perfect, thank you," she said ; "and I have no voice. It is Miss Trenet on whom all our hopes centre ; but Miss Trenet has at present a disagreeable trick of building up hopes one day, and destroying them the next."

"How can you say so !" exclaimed Madame, in thick gutturals ; then addressing Mr. Merrich she went on, " Our Annie has not much look of being one day a singer professional."

"No," he answered, slowly, casting at the same time a curious glance at my unlikely person ; "no. I never was more deceived in my life. I certainly concluded—I should have said decidedly——"

"And you would have said aright," I interrupted. "Herr Droigel told me a story a little time since of a voice which was sent in mistake to the wrong person. Mine is a similar case. No owner has as yet come to claim my voice ; but I am quite certain it does not rightly belong to me."

" There is papa !" exclaimed Gretchen, rising and going out to meet him. She was not a second away, but I knew by her expression when she returned that already Herr Droigel was *au courant* with the whole state of affairs.

Gretchen and I had few reserves in those days.

" What a blessing I chanced to be going out when our worthy landlord appeared !" she said to me afterwards; "and what a mercy papa was not at home and roaming about in that disgraceful old dressing-gown !"

In his town-going costume the father found favour in Mr. Merrich's eyes. He gave his guest a cordial greeting, and desired Gretchen to produce some wine, which had come direct from his own native town of Mayence. Herr Droigel was apt to adopt as his own all towns in which he had ever sojourned. Abroad he always spoke of London as that dear foster-mother, or the English god-mamma who had presented her unworthy child with silver spoons and mugs undeserved.

Whilst he and Mr. Merrich sipped the Marcobrünner, which I do not believe either of them really liked, Gretchen took up the parable of Hayles' enormities.

Herr Droigel listened thoughtfully, and Mr. Merrich looked at me with the entreating eyes of one who should say—

"Pray never tell them the exact contents of that letter."

Perhaps his conscience whispered he ought not to have expected much mercy from me; but I had been for so long a time accustomed to walk overshadowed by Gretchen that I forgave his evident disappointment at my appearance, and answered him with a reassuring glance.

"Ha!" commented Herr Droigel, when Gretchen had finished her narrative, interrupted by idiotic comments from Madame —"ha, I will be one with the sorry rogue some day."

He was holding his glass between himself and the light, and looking at the wine it contained with one eye shut as he delivered himself of this statement, altogether presenting a ludicrous appearance ; and yet spite of the absurdity of his expression and the moderation of his speech, it occurred to me, and also I think to Mr. Merrich, that he would be as good as his word.

Ere long he asked our landlord if he would join him in a cigar, and for some half an hour the pair paced up and down the lawn on which the drawing-room windows opened, whilst Gretchen busied herself with some coloured wool-work, which formed a pleasant contrast to her white fingers ; and Madame, weary of her tight-fitting dress and longing to be out of it, sat down in an easy-chair, and gave utterance at intervals to heart-breaking sighs.

As for me, I began to copy the little song to which I had taken such a fancy. It was contained in a great cumbersome volume, troublesome to lift and place properly on the piano, and I wished to have it in some more accessible form.

"Are not you getting sick of music, Annie?" asked Miss Gretchen at length, smothering a yawn as she put her question.

"Yes, of my own," I replied.

"Why do you not ask your second parent when he intends to give his adopted child a chance of making use of all she has acquired?"

"I have asked him, and he says he does not know—that when the wave comes in we must go out upon it."

"What an utterance!" exclaimed Gretchen, and she resumed her work in silence.

After a pause, she began again—

"Annie, do use another pen or else a pencil; that scratching makes me feel so irritable. I should like to get up and pull your hair."

" You were more amiable at luncheon," I observed, making the exchange she requested.

" Oh, of course ; one had to be agreeable. One did not want to be turned out of the house and with ignominy ; but I declare, what with the shock of meeting that strange individual, and the anguish I endured in making my mother more presentable, and the trouble it was to induce Susan to bring in the dishes and take herself away, I feel quite worn out."

" You look worn out, Gretchen," I agreed ; " your eyes are heavy and your cheeks pale."

" Nonsense," she interrupted, turning sharply round to catch a glimpse of herself in a mirror ; " what a little story-teller you are, Annie !"

" Nay, it was you who said you were worn out," I remonstrated.

" But you said I looked worn out," she retorted.

"I think the one statement was about as true as the other," was my answer.

"Having settled that to your own satisfaction, what do you think of Mr. Merrich?"

"I do not think much of him either for good or for evil," I answered. "I think he is like most people—there is very little in him either to praise or blame. He appears to me——"

"Hush," cried Gretchen, "here they come;" and she bent her head over her many-coloured wools, and I went on with my copying, and Madame raised herself in her chair, grasping the arms with both hands; and the steps came nearer, nearer, crunching over the gravel.

It is hard to tell why some days stand out so much more clearly in one's memory than others—days marked by no special incident, distinguished apparently by no circumstance calculated to impress itself on the recollection—and yet the years gone by contain such for each and all of us. Dreaming by the firelight, looking out over the sea, resting on the green hill-side, wandering through the woods, loitering as the rivulet winds its devious way, singing its low song to the bending ferns and grasses—some days, some hours, for no reason that we can discover, come forth from the recesses of the past and are present with us once again.

The day of Mr. Merrich's visit was one of those marked in my life, and I never could tell why, since the man exercised no influence on my future.

Sometimes I have fancied that, as coming events cast their shadows before, so, when unconsciously our feet cross a fresh boundary and our circumstances enter a fresh epoch of experience, a subtle instinct stamps the seemingly unimportant moment on our minds. That, at any rate, is the only reason I can give why the little room, occupied as I have described, is still present to my mental vision—why the sound of heavy footsteps treading loose gravel underfoot comes back as though my ear were listening to it now.

The footsteps drew near, then stopped outside the first window, through which Mr. Merrich entered, followed by Herr Droigel.

"He said good-bye with much regret," he was kind enough to assure us. "He had spent a delightful afternoon;" this I thoroughly believed. "He hoped he should have the pleasure at some not remote period of seeing us all in Devonshire;" and in conclusion, when the time came for taking leave especially of me, he held my hand for a moment whilst wishing me every success in my profession.

I know now what was passing in his mind. He thought it just on the cards that one day—who could tell?—even poor little I might do something, be a somebody.

The chance was remote; but the way in

which fortune deals out unexpected honours to unlikely people is remarkable, so it was worth while being civil—worth while, spite of the shrug of his shoulders and shake of his head, reflected in one of Mr. Merrich's own mirrors, I caught sight of Herr Droigel executing for his guest's private information.

After this fashion the talk tended, I knew, as the Professor attended his guest to the outer gate—

"She has a little voice, this Annie, so dear to us all ; and if she rest much and take care of her health, and acquires courage and makes friends—who knows ?—she may have a moderate success. Let us hope so."

For me, the time when shrug or shake of my master's could seriously impress or depress me had gone by. I had lived too long behind the scenes for the trick and mannerisms of that actor to impress me painfully ; and so, with a mind uninfluenced by the dismal fiasco that shrug and shake were meant to shadow forth, I returned to my copying, while Gretchen went upstairs to equip herself once more in walking-costume, and Madame hurried after to change her black-silk dress for a déshabille that proved the more distressing by dint of contrast with the fine feathers in which Gretchen had decked her.

As for Herr Droigel, when next he appeared it was in an old pair of trousers, the dressing-gown abhorrent to myself and Gretchen, a waistcoat unbuttoned, and in lieu of cravat an old red handkerchief twisted round his neck. On his head he wore a battered straw hat, which he ceremoniously removed on entering the drawing-room.

"Annie, my child, I absolve you from lessons this afternoon. I go to make myself a sash——"

"A what, Herr?" I inquired, looking in his face, which beamed with pleasure and excitement.

"A glass—how do you call it?—this——"

"Oh, a window sash. What in the world do you want that for?"

"I want to grow myself more salad—more green meats, more lettuce stuff, more everything."

"Then you are going to make a cucumber frame?"

"Thou hast it, Annie beloved—a cucumber frame. You will marvel to see what I plant in it. There, I must hurry away. Be good and practise. Farewell, dear child." And kissing his hand he departed.

I had finished my copying by this time, and was not sorry to occupy the next hour in learning the song.

Simple and easy as was the air, I could not satisfy myself as to the manner of its performance.

Rarely had I been so taken with a melody. It was graceful, it was charming; further, it was all my own. I had never seen it before. Never heard it. Never heard of it.

Possibly had Herr Droigel set me the task I might not have cared to complete it. As the matter stood, I worked at that song. I sang it over and over and over. I tried it in one time and another. I changed the key. I experimented with this expression and with that; and when twilight came I knew it perfectly. I could sit in the dark and let the notes flash out— rising, falling, coming, going, whilst my hands touched the keys lightly, softly indicating an accompaniment rather than playing one.

That night at supper Herr Droigel said to me, "What was it I heard you singing all by yourself with no light in the room?"

"She has been at it all day," explained Gretchen; "a horrid stupid thing. I am sick of the melody, if it have one."

"Will you be quiet, Miss?" exclaimed her father, with more asperity than he usually evinced towards beautiful golden-haired Gretchen. "I addressed my question to Annie, not to you."

"I daresay——" Gretchen was beginning, but I broke across her speech by saying—

"It is a little song of Mozart's."

"Nonsense! Absurd! You talk without understanding!" cried the Professor.

"I assure you it is by Mozart."

"Then I say no; or if yes, you have singed him wrong." When excited Herr Droigel's English was peculiar.

"I sung it right," I answered sturdily. "I have been practising it all day, off and on."

"Then come with me at once." And he rose, and seizing a candle proceeded towards the door, I following.

"Papa, there is macaroni!" called out Gretchen.

"Droigel, Annie goes off leaving her unfinished supper," expostulated Madame.

What Herr Droigel said in reply to both observations it is not for me to repeat *in extenso*. All I know is that an avalanche of German words were preceded by a very English "damn," which I understood to apply especially to his macaroni and my supper.

By the time the objurgation was finished, we had reached the drawing-room and the piano.

" Now for your Mozart, Miss," said Herr Droigel, putting down the candle with a bang.

I did not amuse him with my manuscript, over which I knew he would have pished and pshawed, but I opened the great volume and placed it before him at a distant table, whither I carried the candle.

"Shall I sing it, sir?" I inquired. "*I* know it without the notes."

He motioned me to begin, and I sang it through just as I had done to myself—just as I was able so seldom to sing to him—

with my very soul making melody through
my lips.

When I had done I looked towards Herr
Droigel. Unmindful of macaroni, he was
gazing at the text.

" Oh, thou false Mozart, to have served
me such a trick !" he cried,—" Mozart,
whom I worship ; who stands third only
amongst the musicians I adore ! Thou
faithless Mozart, to thy turns of expression,
to thy marvellous melodies, to thy simple
surprises I could have sworn, I should have
said, so long as hearing remained with me.
But here is something which being yours is
not yours, which comes stealing to me
through the darkness, saying, ' Droigel,
here is an air you are ignorant of, and that
you should know.' Annie, you sing that
melody divinely. Come and let me embrace
you, my child."

Which it is right to say was entirely a
façon de parler on the part of my in-
structor. If ever I went near him after

such a command, he merely took two of my fingers and squeezed them.

On the present occasion we went through this ceremony solemnly ; then after wiping his eyes, he said to me, " I forgot to tell you a piece of news that will please you. We, you and I, are invited to a grand party."

" To a grand party !" I repeated, in amazement. I had heard of such things, but had never been asked to one in my life.

" Yes, where my Annie will have the chance of meeting a select company if she likes to go."

" Tell me all about it," I entreated, my cheeks aglow, my head on fire.

" There is nothing more to tell. We are asked to Sir Brooks' for the twenty-sixth."

" Sir Brooks what ?" I asked.

" Sir Brooks himself," he answered.

Later on in life, I discovered Herr Droigel, clever as he was, never could master the fact that in England the proper names of knights and baronets are not pronounced without a Christian name preceding them.

The " Sir Brooks" we were invited to visit was, in our idiom, Sir Thomas Brooks, Baronet, of No. ——, Park Lane.

END OF VOL. II.

www.ingramcontent.com/pod-product-compliance
Lightning Source LLC
Chambersburg PA
CBHW020945030726
47496CB00005B/1354